DOGS OF A STRANGE TOWN
(Book 3: The Newfie-Bullet Trilogy)

by
William Gough

128 PAGES

ISBN: 978-1-927046-39-5

A Gull Pond Book

Cover: "Hollywood Nor'Wester" ©2016 William Gough
Author Photo: Bill at 5 - Family Album.
Gull Pond Books Logo – Bronson Smith

Dogs Of A Strange Town

(Book 3: The Newfie-Bullet Trilogy)

by

William Gough

gull pond books

For
Caren Moon
&
for my Sister Bev (Gough) Glover
&
for my Mother
Ruby L. Gough
May 5th, 1923-June 13th, 2016

The Gargoyle Descends:

Piano Island:
Uterine life of a Gargoyle:

1: Subjective Shot:

The ocean horizon bends beneath the sky. You recall Piano Island & as soon as you remember, you're back on board. You'd yell but your mouth is glued shut by sheet music, your fingers are stuck to keys.

A distant train-whistle sounds. Tri-note. The Newfie Bullet can float. Narrow-Gage slamming of wheels to tracks. Strange dogs run beside the eternal train.

2: Wide Shot:

Our small baby (born the first time in a tuxedo) is swaddled in black and white. A bow-tie wraps round his neck like an umbilical cord. Wrapped by day & night. The piano roll is click-clicking metallic-hedgehog-music spinning; the paddle wheel's turning & churning the waves, as piano island moves beneath the applauding sky.

3: Ad Hoc Shots:

Wind tugs your hair strands, stretches you, gives you legs. Kelp hair. Peeled legs.

Piano Island floats on a jellied ocean.

Piano Island has three palm trees.

Piano Island has wooden arms.

Wooden arms hold the baby, keeping him from falling into his mother's eyes. From falling through his father's eyes.

Sunlight plays hot upon the wires. Salt crystallizes on the keyboard. Waves make wires hum.

When night comes, the moon holds this baby while the piano plays a lullaby. From a distant ledge, the Gargoyle Poet watches.

Morning returns & the sun crisps the piano. Crusts our tuxedoed baby.

Listen inside your heartbeat & you will hear the songs both the moon & Piano Island sing to this baby. The Gargoyle hums; throat vibrating.

Piano Island floats over a cellophane sea towards our island. Puppet piano baby is tinkling the ivories.

Blood drops.

On the isthmus we're made of meat and music, born with sawdust on our feet. Glued to our mothers for a while, we fall into the angles of our father's eyes & they look anywhere but where we are.

Glued to our mothers for a while, we look into our mother's eyes & out the other side.

Breezes are cold & no one told us we're made of meat and music. The heat has fingers, the sun has nails. I see the sails white on blue. People are walking, sleeping – sometimes both at the same time. Dogs chase sunset. A newspaper blows across the boardwalk. A distant train is smoking. Clouds rise.

You touch my hand.

Sometimes I forget we are made of meat and music.

Cold days on the moon. I smile & for a while, I see you, sawdust on your feet, moondust blowing through your hair; stars beneath your fingernails, reflected in your eyes. Waiting for hands to hold cups & for lips to hold kisses.

The piano stop-frames the sand of meat island, dunes foamed with coral bone. That sand. It grinds open-eyed gargoyles.

Our eyes spill night time, as I claw the sand free & with my floating piano, scoop stars from the shadows near the wires.

On a summer day of white sails; of a little beach & water, we touch. Each finger's made of meat and music.

You fell into my eyes.

I fell into your eyes.

You fell into my eyes.

We are made of meat and music, born with sawdust on our feet.

Glued to our mothers, glued & hidden from our father's eyes & hidden by the night. My fingers move like fallen stars to dip inside the water. My eyes see distant planets.

A little boy swims inside a piano.

My fingers move fallen stars to dip inside the water.

My eyes see distant planets. The water in the piano spills unto the sand, sand wets & then dries. Tuxedo baby moves. Fingers reach for piano keys.

Glued to our mothers.

 Glued.

Hidden from our father's eyes.

Hidden by the night.

All of us are born this way. The first time.

The Music/ The Gargoyle

Three Tones sound – of a sudden - in a silent night rolling along end-to-end, crisscrossed at the middle, spinning a pinwheel yellow, red, blue, white, black color melting into the yellow foaming sea.

And the music crosses all lands everywhere. At once.

Here…

Now…

Then…

…A pinwheel in a cloaked arm, lifts & stops :: spinning a flapping sky. Mantle of time falling over an abandoned temple where one Gargoyle has been looking up since time stopped.

Waiting, algae eyes; green to the skies. Lichen's sweet Ghee; smoke riding the tail, triangles hit - all nine of them.

And the music is around him/it/me.

Oh, sweet earth. My skin cracks. The dendriting fissures earthquake me :: my knees hurt.

O

I have knees.

O

the

Music.

Gargoyles feel their necks creaking, toes itching. And there is a new sound – an old sound – the clicking of Knitting Needles.

Brioche Knit

An apartment in a creaking mansion.

The clik-on-clik of knitting needles. Low enough to coil around her as Granny Knitwit knits in her room of treasures.

Crows stamp erratic circles into the backyard snow where she's cast homemade crusts. They circle the house as needles clatter to the rhythm of "*Des Sept et Huit.*"

Rich neighbors shudder every time they see a crow crap. The Old Woman is un-named except for her all-purpose moniker of Granny Knitwit. She dreams that one day she'll turn to stone. Slow knitting of herself.

Crows leave the backyard to shit on the rooftops of rich neighbors. Like politics, the crap hardens.

Instead of turning to stone, Granny is knitting people, gargoyles, fish, trains, train tracks, insects, hummingbirds – well, whatever there's a pattern for. If there's no pattern, she'll make one up. She knits all kinds of words, sentences, paragraphs & books & a preposition is something she ends a sentence with. As with many many in her world, she was sent here to knit. And knit she shall. Sometimes she goes to the spinning-wheel & spins galaxies. If the mood hits her, she'll knit a planet of odd rules.

And one day, knows she, all knitters turn to stone.

Turned to stone, she'll be dusted by lichen; bleached and tarred by the sun and acid rain. Being knit into life she was dyed; being dyed she's the color of lichen already.

She wears black, and has a small, white, doily-like lace collar. Her hands are made of scales, and they slide one over another as her fingers knit the world, the sky, the water, and the air. That's what a dream told her to do in the good old days before knitting was invented.

By her.

This dream survives knitting & unraveling.

Now she also knits babies, she floats over Newfoundland in dreams, and her fingers stretch thin like high-altitude clouds. In Carbonear, half-formed babies unravel as she knits them. One...two...three...four...unraveled babies.

She's thousands of years old, and her bones ache; she's tempted by stone. Tickled by train-tracks.

If only Gargoyles could move.

Yes...

...If only they moved.

With that 'if' in place, she knows what will happen: one day a producer from LA would be in town, look way up to the turret of an abandoned Kitsilano home – and before the building flipped, she'd be noticed.

Just in time, as the house was to be dismantled. Her stone statue would be taken to Hollywood, and placed inside a collector's private museum.

Such a modest dream.

She – as millennia passed, was ignored & kept knitting first towards and then past the Mayan cutoff time. Far past. Granny Knitwit was left enough money by her latest mother and father so she could live her life and pay the rent while following her dreams.

Her dream was to turn her room into a shrine – to recreate the life of one of her childhoods on Salt Spring Island. It was the green she sought, and the easy roll of crystal rocks.

So she bought paints, and canvas, and fabric and began to change her room into her version of paradise – and dreamed each night of a voice from the Goddess and that voice helped create the painted-poem of her room. Her 3-d printer was her mind & multitudinous yarns.

Chrone hands remember being a child's hands and do paint with that innocence & her hands remember being an old woman who knew the world and those grown-up hands once painted with the sophistication of one who did live a city-life in the city-world. Even with paint she was knitting. It was all she knew how to do – create & destroy. But, those two things kept her going. She bakes Brioche letters. Letters of Challah.

She calls on her friends of the city, those who live in the streets and those who live in small rented-by-the-day or rented-by-the-week rooms.

Together they gather poems, they collect sounds, they make the world become the way they want the world to be, and the room becomes a rainforest room. It bends stone images; reflects city life & echoes of discarded hub-caps & clang-a-ways. She knits a ghost-train.

The paintings:

Each is inside a grotto-indented shrine. At the foot of some paintings, sand-boxes with votive candles are enclosed in glass with slots so as to catch letters on fire! In the sand, granulated paintings of words and images are left incomplete in only one small detail.

The poems:

Some poems Granny Knitwit baked out of bread in her small oven, and set out to be read in Challah-twists of words. They were glazed like baker's show-case breads, and set on rough wood shelves made of biscuit boxes from forgotten childhoods. This wood she painted. She knows your favorite colors and dips her brush inside your mind.

The room:

The room was made into a forest. Dry wood – driftwood, logs reclaimed from the ocean, dried seaweed tangled. Vines link, and gauze material has light-poems stuck to it. The room is soft, with knitted walls; filled with dappled light.

The sounds:

Music – composed by her street-friends & performed by buskers falling through the cracks & crashing on the streets & reverse-film while standing up playing their instruments for pennies. Think of people with fiddles, accordions, harps, & Chinese Violins. Musicians dancing & playing & and singing on street corners & helping her re-create the room & they lend their voices and carvings to this room. Tri-Note whistle.

Stone:

Her door opens into a forest-swathed entrance that leads to the poem rooms. Granny keeps knitting – awaiting the gargoyles and their children. They bring stone to life.

> She knits stone to life.
> She knits life to stones.
> She knits life.
> This is the place where she knits all her worlds.

Piano Childhood:

We help her create the sheet music. Easy to find – we tear it from our lips. There's a little bleeding – a second birth. On sea legs, we long for stone legs. On solid legs, we wobble on earth towards the piano.

We all arrive from small rooms of a meat-island childhood & like sea-saws we limp down the hallway. Our foot prints are red on black & white tiles. Our eyes project light. We pray for stedi-cam eyes.

Down the long hall is where the piano is – where music lives.

Placing the sheet music so burning torches catch the nite-notes, the libretto is revealed.

Our eyes no longer baby eyes, our eyes no longer nite-light eyes, we see :: we read.

In the beginning sing these words:

Before we get up, the bed is springtime warm.

When we got up (footprints in warm hall sand) the bed held the imprint of our bodies. Later, the bed cools & flattens.

No sign anyone ever slept there.

The wind blows sand. The bed stays cool. Sometimes it's *now*, sometimes *then*. Same time.

Life is a piece of cake. Make no mistake about that. We thought it was caught & held. A ball in blue and brown rolling down. An easy catch for you and me. Sure.

I have a secret.

Hide with me in the forest where everyone walks naked. Hide with me in the forest that everyone tries to clothe.

My body is the dog that won't be muzzled; the itch that can't be scratched; the pig that eats the truffles. When I go walking in the forest it will not come quietly. It snaps at twigs, eats small scared animals, and pisses on the trees.

Sometimes it scrapes leaves off shallow graves.

I'm older than a gargoyle. I stare at you. I have crooked teeth and peer into the sun. My glasses shine. With all the time in the world, my loonie-store glasses angle sunlight into your eyes. My coat is blue. I made it from a pattern. I wear suit-pants made from patterns & tissue paper folded. I cut and I sew. My back is bent – my spine is a bent coat-hanger.

I stare at you.

Your car shines sun at me. The sound of tires drifts my way. You look my way. I shine the sun at you. The air is hot outside your car. My coat is missing one button. Your locks click - the sun fits everyone. It's hot outside your car, I stare at you.

I stare at everyone.

I have crooked teeth & peer into the sun. As I look your way, my glasses shine.

Echo again; Life was a piece of cake. Make no mistake about that, we thought it was caught and held, a ball in blue & brown rolling down.

When I first joined the army that's what I thought. I still wear putties. I must always wear a baseball glove. The sun's an easy catch for me.

When I'm not catching planets, I work in the people factory. Sometimes I make mistakes. Who doesn't make mistakes? Not me.

Make a big mistake & they turn you into a Gargoyle. Or three or six. All the same.

Regular chorus line of gargoyles, step-strobe-kicking, eyes upwards, or downwards.

Cement doors open.

Crypt-lids: open-life.

Gargoyle clam shells part.

All at once, the music, Flapper style, all of us the one Gargoyle mother/father/children.

At once the lids give birth to rows of us, lifted by the crane of the skies. Back to our necessary rows. Atop the world, waiting. No more

Home.

Work.

We needed to make Gargoyles because there was one big mistake we made. Long years ago in the people factory.

Various mistakes:
The need for Gargoyles to make babies:

Our mistake meant no bones were planted in that year's planting season & this year's cluster of people still lies jellied in the vat.

It's not like carving marble.

People-jelly wobbles in the light & waits to sense brother-seeds & sister-seeds bobbing along; red-red-robins to keep them company; to give them comfort, for they are alone.

Features almost formed do bounce against the light. My stone feet click down the sparbled stairs. A whirlpool swim of faces greets me at the gate, swimming whirlpools narrow as a manta-ray slides beneath floating oranges spilled from an ocean liner in harvest season.

Hear the echo. Hear the beating of my chambered heart.

A small boy is swimming in the jelly-rolled-piano, he has brought shells with him & when he dives to the bottom of the piano, he scrapes the wires. Shells make them sing. Bubbles leak from his mouth, up the treble clef, rising to pop notes on the surface.

The moon sneaks into his room to accompany him but, noticing the boy plays deep inside the piano, is content to bend and hit the saw & hum along with popping bubbles.

This boy does not need to breathe - he sucks water in through his teeth & squeezes all the moisture out. He holds air deep in his lungs.

His hands float towards the surface & when he follows, his floating phalanges rise in the water. His fingers spread as wide as the sky; nails glint silver as the moon. All piano keys spill between his outstretched-fingers & he holds music by its slippery tail.

For a while, he lies upon the music like a surfboard but then dives again deeper & deeper, further away from those who say "You can't!

You will!

Not you..."

All that remains within his ears is the sweet water of music - the press of waves & bubbles filling his eyes.

A boy - a small boy - is swimming in the piano.

Jelly fish sleep on propeller blades. A swimmer's bare feet sink into pin-pricking sea urchins. The sea worm draped across a rock is sucked by undertow, is undulated by ocean waves.

An eel slides on his open eye.

Piano daze/Gargoyle days:

Wind. Low tide.

Earth shows, beach shows, road shows, city shows.

Old Gargoyles balance on a rooftop.

Old people at street-level balance their heads along a fence to watch a building being built by those who have no time to watch.

Heads bob - a row of pumice-puffballs in the sun.

Roar of traffic-wind counting time by bristles. Extra eyebrow hairs do flutter along the faces of the heads balanced on a fence. Heads stop nodding when naked puffballs say the day is done.

Years float Piano Boy over the land, around a cloud & he's gravity-hooked to earth. Earth tides move him thru years. Years flip him to his feet. His fingers ripple.

Clinging to the roof, the Piano Gargoyle looks down.

Passion is spent before the moment goes round the corner; there's no belief in a love that's new or even one that will do 'till the right one comes along.

Air quivers in the heat. Enough to cook the egg upon the sidewalk. Humans playing in the street wonder if what Ozymandias said was true.

They count –

One, Two, three.

Skip.

Two by two they count:

Mabel, Mabel set the table.

Skip.

Don't forget the pepper and salt.

 Skip/ Slap/ Skip/ Slap.

Skipping ropes.

Take a nap & dream that horses are tied up along the sidewalk. Not yet time to stampede along the shoreline, grow sharp teeth and look for humans to bite past life. Before that time. Lean, razor-toothed dogs, angle and circle, around and around.

Teeth flash sun. Tails down. Across the beach a car, surrounded by dead babies, skids across the sand & towards Carbonear.

See the horses, watching dogs, listening to crying babies all over the world. Smells of horse-shit in hundreds of Gargoyle cities, hoof caves dug deep into a beach. Crescent ponds. In cities even the ponies are wall-eyed, wall-leaning.

One eye looks at humans. One eye (towards the sky) sees Gargoyles watching. Watching both, the Poet-Gargoyle is very still. Piano-Gargoyles are quiet.

They sometimes dream of the days when oranges were wrapped in purple paper billowing around the edge of crates. Santa Gargoyle would squeeze and the oranges would roll to each, through doors and into waiting stockings. Then the oranges would wrap themselves into beds of paper.

Make no mistake about it – winter's been & gone & the summer's come & we're all undone. A memory Train click-clacks on mind-tracks.

Make no mistake.

One Gargoyle Descends.
While another Gargoyle is born:

On my first journey along the road, the dust covers me, like a flag of color, rippling my stone flesh.

&

I find a school where no one is sure which of the students has stolen whatever's gone from its accustomed place. A necessary situation in the life of objects.

All teachers are sure something's gone. No specifics, mind, but on this chalk-filled morning something's missing.

"Analyze the dust" is the suggestion of the chemistry master.

"Analyze the dust," in wonder, murmurs stuffed uniforms gathering near the leaning fence, near the old out-house tilting near the bank.

Scuttlebutt has it that one piano boy had worn a large white hat for that morning (that morning only) & had placed in his locker, next to the old sheet music, the tatters of that hat.

I am a gargoyle; all of us, stone men & rock women, have a womb of shale; a cave held inside each of us like air is held inside yr closed fist.

Home.

Smoking home detectives, solving cases of accidental life. Holding magnifying glasses, stalking corridors; Gargoyle toes on stone floors.

Back in the 14th century before freeze-bombs and heat bombs, before our time when worlds are ending for flesh-pods, when all Gargoyles go to crypts, and mummies clank as Mother drags stone blankets over our head; this time the soft ones melt.

Just before (with time-spill we walk over the worlds, blasted occasionally.) Boom. Soon as the soft ones awaken, they make bombs and kill each other.

They snow-whited into sleep until a gargoyle princess kissed them all. Shaken from a dream, they walk again.

All the dead ones think they are awake, have lives, vote, don't vote. Pass motions, run facebook, eat, buy, cry themselves asleep. Invent shit.

Even a gargoyle heart cracks with sorrow from walking thru dreams & moving & singing, shaking hands with each other, hugging, going to strip shows, playing pool, running down the street, robbing each other in empty streets.

The usual.

O as soon as they snow-white into life, they simply resume things, ignoring that, in the missing second, the world has blown up, re-formed & once again, put all of us stone-angels back on row after row in Dollar Stores, as if there were just a missing nano-second.

O, as soon as they blip back into time, they recommence killing each other, for the soft ones scare easily. Missing links with lasers.

Being Gargoyle-born, never sleeping; always knowing just how close we are to the black hole, we long to stretch in lava stone; are waiting to melt again & swim with Pele.

As a Gargoyle-poet, a detective of stone, and being Granny Knitwitted into life's sweater, I decide to investigate. Waiting till the candle flings deeper shadows against the velvet yellow & as each brown curl of wallpaper quivers, I hesitate for a very long time.

Investigating Gargoyles always know how to wait. We make poems – we become detectives.

O, I'll wait until the last slippered foot has slapped the lino in the hall.

O, I'll wait until the last card of the masters hits the table between the wisp of hands and the shuffling of cards.

"O," said I, "I'll wait."

The dust that densed my still-life, stopped its roll down the mountain of apples and pears.

I try to move softly, to make no noise (for a Gargoyle this is never easy). Sometimes it takes a year or two to advance along one shadowed hall.

Gargoyles live in all tenses, what they call past, present and future. Fuck that. I put all tenses into the word-mixmaster's bowl of stone. Drink that, soft ones. I grind words with my stone heel. Crows pick letters off when I sleep (toes up) as part of a cliff.

I wait until there's a lull of a year or two – a school bankruptcy, I believe; new investors needed to be found, new suckers.

It's always a relief when the halls are empty.

Then, and only then, I stomp down the hall towards the large dormitory where seniors are permitted to store cherished trophies in their lockers. The prisons of learning always include numbered lockers.

Green light hangs near the ceiling & in folds across the beds. Night-time quiet makes the room dry as bronzed lemons.

When I sit down on a buckling bench, the wood dents & creaks as, at all the other school-desks, students get up, go to one locker & lift out a saran-wrapped *something* slipping inside the wraps. It drips from near the feet to echo lights upon the floor (a light of red and sheen.)

Believing they're observing a miracle instead of the everyday sight of a gargoyle walking, at first they approach and kneel and light candles, you know – God stuff. Naturally, I stayed very still, for that always works.

In my stillness I see with wide-eyes, unblinking-eyes, stone-teared-eyes, exactly what gift they bring.

They carry tapers and one still baby from a piano.

Ripping it from the hook (the butcher's hook) where it had hung to (game-like) ripen, they slide it onto a table near my bending bench – O, what a skinned grape of a boy.

Because of what happens when I still my heart, my chest, my eyes, my restless plumed & hoofed legs. Because of what happens when I keep my vision still; because of my being motionless, they feel safe and touch my shoulder.

Because of that, the dead may, once again, live.

Very still, peeled human, I coat you with my still eyes, I let my stone heart beat once – twice – thrice.

The still boy is still no more.

All hold their breath; the breath of wood and boys & this is what's on the first turning of the road… He speaks.

Tho' all hear, he speaks to me.

"O," he says, says he, "There are not many of us who floated through the bubbles intact. When bubbles sheened the frog-shape head, the blood-twisted turnip with legs wound over & through the cris-cross twins growing from the same stomach, we piano kids were flung into the sky. Smashed against the rocks, we rode the monorail to the moon. We formed within a floating piano.

We then descended to earth where we were often eaten, taught piano, or peeled and hung on butcher's hooks – sometimes a combination of all. You know, human-beings gobbling up all animal-beings. The 'eat-the-other-aliens' approach that defective simians use.

Sometimes, for amusement, humans exhibited us in traveling shows. This began to happen after influenza raked across earth like a fine toothed comb. That time when there was the great joining, the hidden corporations merging with the so-called 'real' countries. That was the time of religions & butcher shops – our time of the great alliance. Meat-eaters & meat-breeders & meat-jugglers – that alliance.

I floated in a bell jar, deep in the dimmed freak show. The

holes above my ears held words like hard tight plums, echoed the Carney-bark & then pointed dolphins out to sea.

Under the farmer's gaze - the legless boy & the armless girl.

The head without a body is my kin & I dance while in the sea-weed, in the reeds of riverbank under my clapping stone feet - above the storm sewer, the tide rubs along the distort - blurring your lens in the waves."

Those are the first words of the still boy.

I have only one reply & my jaws unwired, the creaking makes the students move to the shelter of the walls. My voice rolls words of dust to fill the room, halo lamps, grit eyes – schoolboy gargoyles. I speak what it was I knew – "I rescue us."

O, baby Gargoyle boy, my dust lies on your raw flesh like a mantle. It micro-dots and holds, red at first in the first layer of word-dust.

And then another layer of words: "I rescue them."

The next layer grits and holds, forms stone flesh. I see a stone boy, his flesh made marble. Marble dust. I swear his lips can move again.

Stone lips. Carved teeth & dust-on-dust, he speaks once more.

Dust-words cloud the room. The dead live.

He speaks again.

"Split-open faces are lying on the river bottom where pebble-babies hear the sound of those smashed on desert rocks.

See slow motion unveiling of bone caves, of cities of the cells. The gray glacier of the brain rolls down the rocks."

My child is born.

A capelin cloud of babies has dusted to our town & one is lying in a bed of sand.

Gargoyle birth is never easy. Chisel-cut after hammer-stroke, stone bleeds mud.

Gargoyle-boy Speaks the Language of Dust:

I lift my self to the floor. On wobbly legs I walk. Water drips off me and to the floor, I am together. I am my self. I visit you.

In your attic, eggs are resting on an anvil.

Eyeballs press against shattered dormer panes.

You offer yet another cup of tea and, as you pour, waves ride through the shell.

Glass beads are rapids-riding in my veins so I must sit very still.

On a peeling steamer trunk, plums are rotting in a cut-glass dish.

O, the wedding cake is crumbling in the palace of the mouse. Tiny beads have tarnished near the edge. Through the cracked window, carriage ruts do pyramid the frost into a crazed and rigid glazing.

Pip is small & Pip is in the hand that holds the shadows. I am born of words. I pop again into the world. An unexpected crumble, I fall from cake already on your lips.

I am lonely for the roof. I turn slowly, past the frozen boys, past the dust of powdered snot & tears & I follow father to the roof.

The roof takes a year's travel to reach, but is worth it & slates fall in an acute tipping & I am home. Home with eves-troughs. What boy could want more?

"You are," says Father, "Pip. You are a marble-Pip & the world will roll us. The world is a marble. We bounce like Pinballs & we bounce in this world."

Sometimes, now, I see – as if insects in a blur, school-boys aging & leaving and returning, stone-haired.

Once in a while they look up – so fast. Mayflies all, they die. Some are burned & scattered and we hold their dust in our arms, finally the dust blows from our shoulders, our unblinking eyes.

Day and night are two cars in a fast train on a short circle of track. Narrow gage.

At first I was dizzy, now I am simply…

… gargoyle.

Gargoyle at a piano.

Piano gargoyles sing in a gargoyle lounge:
He meets his first mama:

Earth Mama:

I hungered. A shell - frog-like - was hidden.
Flicked my tongue, in our vase, to fix the flying, white flecks of/ shards of/ glass./ Glass exploded across/exploded across/\ the room/ \across the room.

Earth Papa:

You were/ not hit/ because I killed/ the glass/ instead/ of you/ exploded near the/\ corner of the room.

Earth Papa/Earth Mama:

(singing together)

Now, little Gargoyle Boy, creak down to earth & work for us.

Vegetable Talk

(His human upbringing. Where still boys are born so they may die)

Vegetables are imprisoned everywhere; gripped by earth. Roots are locked by earth, waiting to get into the air. They live in rootdom, talking to one another from their tight prisons of clay and humus.

They talk over rotted logs that are too old to speak anymore & they speak to the fungus. Only occasionally, however, because fungus always wants to know:

"Who's here? How long will you stay?

&

May we join you?"

At one time, the social lives of vegetables were wonder-filled, for, indiscriminately, they'd all be scattered in a field. Sometimes a radish would nestle next to an ear of corn, beside the radish next to them there'd be onions drinking all night...

... *Gimmie a brew* they'd say, *anyone got a smoke? Anyone got arms? I want a smoke.*

... Carrots would drop by & they'd stay, just move in, green hair tickled in full moonlight. No one ever said there must be no carrots in this field.

One day, they started to specialize. Onions spoke only to other onions, speaking the same language – (a variation of Tuber) They do not speak broccoli, they do not speak the sweet cloying language of plums. And plum is the only language I know. For, a long time ago, when I was a little boy, someone mailed me a rotted blue plum.

This is significant only in that, yesterday, after I had pried up the covers, stirred strongly & smelled the swirl of cobalt paint against wood, I then left the painting to my assistant, a simple man who always left his fingerprints on Scotch bottles.

I went home to see my family, but instead opened the mail – where there was a rotted plum in a parcel. For a moment I thought I was on my parents' old tape of Sesame Street, and I was privileged, perhaps pleasantly, to present (perfectly) the letter 'P.'

Hmmmm - A plum in a parcel & I looked out and said "Please Postman, pungent plums in a package, Pourqui?"

No letter 'P' materialized. The Postman hurried away, with a terse "piss-head!".

It was a quiet, solemn day; an undertakers' day.

A day of absolute calm - neighbors gathering in all their houses, because they knew of this arrival of the parcel & the plum in the parcel - the rotted plum from childhood - they knew of it long before I did.

I could see (behind curtains' eyes) binoculars, telescopes, optical creations of all manner & neighbors' eyes behind them.

They thought they were invisible to me.

In the mail there'd come for me a parcel wrapped in oilskin. When I opened the package, there was the smell of plum and clouds. When the oilskin was opened, mist cupped me & crowned me; held me until I was rising above the earth.

Deep back on earth outside my house, there was one painter & he held a brush up to paint the sky blue & the paint leaked down over his wrist. I had not known how blue the skies could be.

The vegetables sang and I sang. With each note, with every word, I floated clear of the sky, until I had nothing else to do except light the cloud until it blazed & pinned each blazing moment of light against the deep black of what was only the memory of the curtains of my baby's room.

When visitors rode the Newfie Bullet to the house for dinner all were served vegetables they believed were for eating & gulping down. They didn't know how things worked at our house. For, at the point of swallowing, my parents would go to them and say, "Don't swallow! Don't swallow! Have you no thought for the child? Don't you know of Benjamin, our little baby?"

The guests would mumble replies with their mouth full of unswallowed vegetables.

Well, we still don't know much about Benjamin. I heard he was my brother. The help spoke of this – not to me directly, but they muttered it to the tablecloth.

- We don't either! Don't swallow, don't spit out the vegetables - would say my mother -

Don't swallow - my father would say.

Don't spit it out - my mother would say.

What else can we do? - the guests would mumble.

Their mouths were also filled; green grains falling to the floor.

- Just do what you're doing, until the bowl is fetched. -

And someone would go to fetch the bowl. It was, I'm told, because I was not allowed to dine with our neighbors. All because of what happened to Benjamin. Because of that!

The bowl was green with a gold rim. All the visitors would, only then, on cue, finally spit - not the entire meal, but just the vegetables - the first chomp & chew would be mixed together and then...

"He'll find it like a puppy," they'd say. "He'll find it like a pup."

I have no memory of this. My proof is the bowl itself (which I've seen – again & again & once again & again. Again to infinity.) Vegetables to the nth power. And its use was described as being for something else.

I won't describe what else, because it had to do with death & it had to do with bludgeoning.

But, it certainly had very little to do with vegetables at that time.

Vegetables?

Okay, it was done for color as well.

In my memory of the curtained life, there were carrots. Carrots for the exquisite orange & the way chewed carrots would hit the green & then dry like failed knitting.

My parents were very interested in art. They were always interested in culture and, because they were, it left me a legacy - through vegetables - of art that is never to leave me.

Now I've been told that the only function of art is to be serious, to make one feel agony & I ask - how can masticating vegetables & spitting them - with a warm phutie, into bowls, create agony?

This was back in the fifties, so they weren't quite as advanced in social etiquette as we are - but, I understand they would, at the end of the day, take off their shoes and socks. The bowl wasn't quite big enough to stand in & stamp the cooked cold vegetables down, but it was large enough to accommodate up to a size thirteen foot which was pretty substantial.

People in those days had smaller feet. For some reason (I don't know why) they had tiny toes. Large feet weren't required & people hadn't evolved to the stage of today, where sometimes, size 15, triple E, is common for little girls and boys. Some adult clowns, I've been told, have feet now that are the size of surf-boards. These people live in Malibu & chase rats - that's what they're hired to do.

Rat-chasing clowns? Keep yr eyes open and you'll see them.

Back in the day of my childhood – those far-ago days, vegetables were chewed and spat into the bowl – "Will he find it?" was the question. "Will we see him become a puppy and find it?" (As an aside) how can this be agony in art - a warm bowl, filled with fresh & slipping vegetable mash, leaned over by a boy who's learning to be a puppy?

 Of course not, for art is never agony. That's what pebbles say.

- Will we see him be a puppy? - guests ask again.

No one ever sees him - replied my mother. He lives in a room on the third floor, a room of many curtains & those multi-colored curtains thwart his movement, so he heads for the window - to climb out. But, sadly, he becomes entangled in the drapes.

Tradition had it that, when the bowl was left in my room I would - swaddled in curtains - make my way to the bowl & eat the chewed-up vegetables. It was very simple.

I suppose it was much like anyone's house – that's the way things were done in my place.

I'm told some curtains were gold and green - the color of the bowl, the same color of the bowl we discussed. They would wait...

...The very next day, I fell from my bike, just like Benjamin & lay on my side like an Aztec meteor – (all pinwheels and pyramids) - apologizing to the drivers who had hit me, had knocked me to my side.

Bam.

A couple of bounces thrown in.

Imagine my astonishment when I discovered that the car which bounced me around was driven by my own parents.

They were equally astonished to have hit me & asked what I was doing on the road? Out of my room? Where did I find the bicycle?

I used the opportunity, talking in the rhythm of the ratchet of the spinning bike wheel & asked them about the bowl & if it was normal that I had to live like a puppy & was it true about being a puppy?

No answers.

They took away my bicycle. That night, when I climbed up the drainpipe to the third floor & slipped back in through the curtains. I remembered the bicycle & wondered if I would ever see it again. I let my lips brush against the ribbed fabric, frayed fiberglass drapes & forgot the bicycle till now.

From below the stairs I could hear the sounds of pages turning. There was classical music on the gramophone & I was happy to be in this house where culture-curtains wave brave flags on magically still days.

I hummed along, quietly enough so they would never hear me, yet loudly enough so I'd hear myself and my voice. That voice would one day be as strong as water, as deep as waves. As billowing as a nightshirt that could unfurl in a cloud while I was falling through the cloud. I loved water as much as my Aunt Irene.

That night I dreamed of water, knowing that deep under the water there are creatures, green and orange, like giant goldfish with human faces. They'll nibble the ears of Aztec meteors when fiery rocks do hiss & spit into the ocean or the vegetable dish.

I knew I could be a puppy in the water. Could nuzzle weeds with my muzzle & gurgle my speech about art & about culture. Instead of climbing into a dream, I'd climb into the bed that's hidden in the ocean. I would inhale until weeds tickled enough inside my lungs to grow there & to let me, for the first time in my life, sing.

That sound would not be the song of a puppy.

That tune would hold the vibrations of a green-and-gold being, flying in pyramids through deep waves & whose lungs are always filled with song. I would lie (away from curtains) in water that flowed everywhere in the world.

On that last day when the water covers the tip of the tallest skyscraper.

On that day, when the world smells like an empty aerosol can, I'll sing like Elvis Starr while he plays his interstellar concertina.

On that day when flame marries water, I will float to the surface on my bicycle and see that the only curtains left in the world will be the clouds & they'll always ask me to dinner & I will eat dessert with the sun & together I'll sing with the moon.

We'll sing to each other of the ocean.

Sing to each other of a world without curtains.

Granny Knitwit Knits with dust.
(Back Cross One Over One Over One Knit)

Granny has been knitting a long time – since before she had a head; since before she had hands.

First she had one sharp thought which had no words. That became her first needle.

Next she understood the nature of wool, and the need for sheep. That became fused as her other needle.

When she understands there needs to be a knitter - that's what begins to form her own eyes, her hands, her womb, her ears. That was her life inside the first cave, where she knits (from the dust that is everywhere) her very first world.

Just like that.

Take one thread, tug it through the neck of the bellows, breathe in water, breathe out air; breathe in dust, breathe out fire. Breathe in fire, breathe out water; breathe in water, breathe out us.

And then, a few Gargoyles, knitted from new rock, fold over needles while dust is molten, and we have a world of hidden stone gargoyles.

The first were freed by alchemists with chisels.

Seemed like the work was finished. Gargoyles lived in tilts over Notre Dame; pointed to sigils on the wall, picked their noses in what took forever.

They'd been waiting. Once on their feet, they headed towards partly formed babies; babies lost in the way of the world; discarded children concealed in the shadows of schools, beneath the water of pools, hidden in the ground, left in dumpsters, sold for organs, abandoned in war, marched into the ordered desks of High School, sitting lost in university cafeterias.

Waiting for Hollywood gargoyles.

Waiting for Granny Knitwit to knit life into Gargoyles, into poets, throughout Hollywood. Yarn strung from gorilla mountain to gorilla mountain – the orange sunsets of Vancouver mountains, the hills of gentle and sudden slopes when the smog leaves Pasadena.

And now, as we read, she knits, and fashions of our entwined eye-beams, a grid of light.

And on this new first day it rains, and dust smears over her hands, and along the needles, and as purple yarn it coils around the knitting.

From dust, Granny knits. And from the rust of an old life, we are reformed.

Knit one, purl two.

No longer are we few; now there will be millions of us on our feet and we walk away from banks, and gold, and diamonds, and shiny cars. We know there is a necessary story waiting in each wave, on all the sands, new tides are being knit to light, folded into darkness. We poem-walk. Slowly.

This is the time Gargoyles have dreamed about.

These are the gargoyles that Granny Knitwit has yarned about.

We are, all of us, here.

Time to knit together.

Piano Gargoyle: (Hollywood Lessons)

When they ask you to sit down at the piano, the people who pay piano gargoyles to write music for Hollywood's version of the world, first, they say they will pay for your days. There isn't enough time to look at your wrist-watch.

I have had these people already tell me:

"It's only business."

"We feel the script needs some new energy."

"You're being a bit defensive" they say (standing on your throat) & then, they tell you there's a "bottom line."

Bottom line? My marble butt! Kiss it!

Lesson the second:

Know this; the wind blows cold across their teeth. Their mineral water has lost its fizz; their de-caf has lost its kick. Their diet cola has lost its power to shrink the body past the ribcage.

Each day I paint my skin so I may look human, I plate my chest & slip pneumatic bags deep inside so I appear to breathe. If I did draw breath, dust would fill the room & cover them, encapsulate them, tombstone them.

I could go on, but I long to tinkle Ivories, giving a light touch so I won't gargoyle-crush the piano.

Losing my way I found my way.

Falling I rose. Rotting, I gained weight. Thought of becoming human again.

Father followed me. Disguised in a lounge suit, red-dusted face. Like a walking slab of brick. He scares the shit out of some & others try to take chisels to him. When the chisels break they run, screaming, away.

That's my dad!

Staying still, I moved. I know the empty eyes; empty hearts. But I never have to play the piano in front of those eyes & I never have to sing to ears filled with manicured fingers.

I listen to other piano-gargoyles in lounges all round tinsel town.

I walk Los Angeles streets at night.

By day, producers tell me that they'd like my hands to move a different way. It doesn't matter that I can't see my wrists, for there's money in the bank, and they sleep on it while I write.

They pull greenbacks round their jammies & dream of money riding on my fingers.

If they weren't so scared, they'd truly see my porous fingers. If they weren't so scared, why, blood would leave their ears alone & they'd expect my piano to surf across the red wave, with me as a singing anchor.

They were never really there, even when I thought they were, they weren't – for, to them, all of us are just numbers on the jukebox in a joint too loud to hear the music. You know – jukebox bosses.

Bosses.

Boss.

All the way up the mountain-top where I catch the music & pluck it from deep-night morning, I hear the music & it hears me walking on bending scaffolds. I climb reinforced ladders to small winged moments, while on the ground (they have but one sail on the ground) they have one anchor & it rattles a death-star-money-rattle.

In early morning I sail by in my stone-gondola & play music.

They look at music-clouds & see that clouds are made in their eyes from tiny torn fragments of money & they think sails of music are made of c-notes & they talk tough & they chill & they think it's too slow and they think it's too fast & O, their feet trip in the money & O, they fall off mountains of money & it's a tough life and someone's gotta do it & they're glad people smoke again 'cause they're glad to pretend to be the guy that Bogart pretended he was & they swim in bubbles & they can't hear, cause they don't care.

Bogart was a rich boy but they don't care – he was their idea of tough & he had it down pat. Soft skinned tough guy on the screen.

The fear that keeps them saying 'yes' is what allows them to say 'no'.

They're scared because they have left the world behind and know only hotel suites, where brave men weep tears of silver dollars & where all the brave listen to the news & say 'Jesus,' & spit & piss & talk loud while they piss.

The world collapses, and widows cry.

The wailing of children fills the ears of gargoyles.

The dank air that blows over rotting teeth; the cancer untreated makes soft tissue cauliflower. Microwaves beep. Wi-Fi transmitters mutate us, the ice melts, oceans rise. That time.

There's a line-up for the hospitals that turn us away & ambulances speed through the streets. When there's a traffic jam, it's always filled with ambulances.

On apartment ledges we gargoyles watch the rich send out for the poor. Rich folk eat the poor, have pâté ground from factories. The poor have the poor. The rich cook them with jobs.

Chickens hang upside down by claws waiting for the electric knife. Humans wear see-through raincoats & are paid to use electric knives on live hen necks. Humans have some scattered blood-drops congealed on their shoulders when they go home.

Adjustment.

Blood-drops slo-mo spatter on see-thru vinyl.

Gargoyles' shoulders show the blood.

Humans do all this without noticing the blood showing. All that's left are the buckets gathering flesh & heat-lamp-tables crisping the flesh. Deep fryers deepen flesh & permeate flesh with oil squeezed from swimming aliens.

On this space ship the Captain eats the passengers.

Sometimes we see the rich watch the news. There are no tears; they smile & call their bankers - Jesus, another crash, raise to cost of...well... *everything*. There's money to be made, boys! Forty percent inflation? Hell, let's go for Fifty. The sheep will follow. Rich folk sit in clouds of smoke in front of stock-market feeds, and eat the world with their eyes as fingers. Dip their eyes into the bankers' pockets. They smile and then turn Bogart-tough. Sure. Trumpian failed-bellman echoes. Sure; when their minds grow duller.

That world, those people.

They are week-end hunters (like week-end Presidents) who have lost their guns, but would love to kill the baby & the mother & the father deer & smear deer-blood across their chests to show they have more than magazines in their waiting rooms but their time won't let them, so they can only wound writers & directors & actors & composers & those who answer phones & those who hold dying laptops in the nest of their arms while they, them-very-selves, sleep.

Better not shoot me, you assholes (yep, even Gargoyle-born know how to swear!) – the bullets will bounce back - dum-dum flattened.

Watch out, producers. There are now gargoyle singers, piano-players, dancers, and... there are gargoyle writers.

We see the hearts of humans who wait for text & those who encode files & those who park cars & those who steal cars & those who steal from writers & those who wait for tips & those who hold hats out & those who write about the movies & those who wish to write for the movies & those who hate writing for the movies & wish they could stop.

Humans must content themselves with photos of blood & films where women are wounded, where children work & lose their childhood so (in the dark) people may believe this is the way to the blood-beat; this trail of sharp celluloid; these tree-branches of video.

Audiences swear that Bruce Willes can fall down an elevator shaft & still be a hero & climb walls & then zig-zag into the sunset after having his ass blown off.

Such movies are riotous comedies for gargoyles.

We watch these human mollusks with their bones of shell fall & get up again & we always laugh cause there ain't no suspense in watching pale bodies fall and get up again.

Humans don't get up again. Even worms know this.

Such are the comedies of gargoyles. We laugh when Mayfly humans blur in and talk of eternal sky-gods.

O...Sure!

Might as well write a holy book about atomic-bugs. We'd laugh all night. Fortunately, sirens drown us out.

Here are some of the soft-ones' beliefs & practices:

They must content themselves with eating others while still saying "It's only business." They go to studios so they may tie up writers & composers.

There are those who carry diet-drinks on silver platters & set bodies on fire & watch flames burn thru hearts & watch orange & black singing fingers & wonder why the world is burned-out.

Deep in the honey-money-cloud, they know they can only stay alive if we let them. They can only sleep if we stay awake. They can only dream if we let them steal our own.

"What is there to learn?"

"What may this teach me?"

It's so simple - there's not only one dreamer of this dream -

and dreamers are neither selling nor buying.

You dream a cloud & the cloud is not money.

The cloud is made from piano smoke, from piano fingers, music and heart and dreams & that is something they cannot buy, even when they pay you & that is something they never can buy with stolen dreams.

A miracle has happened!

You were about to walk into the dragon's mouth and he turned away & said he didn't want you.

You were on a cliff & they were going to tie clocks to your still feet.

You were in someone else's ocean.

Now…

… you look at a moon that isn't a silver dollar. You are in the middle of a miracle & no longer standing on the slippery slope of their tin ears and hearts. You are in a tipi in a Salty forest.

In short, you have learned that memos say nothing, that the silica-phone texts magic words, or an assistant to a flunky opens a mollusk-mouth & fish-breathes magic words of liberation:

"We're going to have to let you go."

O, sweet production-codfish, gasp on, my friend. These are the magic words that force all Spells to end.

I am let go & all my dust falls to the ground. The marble turns around, once, twice, thrice.

And I am, at last, let go.

My piano father goes back to the roof. He knows the truth - I have been let go; turned back into flesh.

Not rye, not peeled flesh, not the mere sourdough of a boy – I am, to my joy, able to play with the best-nest-rest of them.

I am filled with blood, and my veins are skeined of wool.

Of Regaining Flesh and Blood:

I slept three decades, three years, three months, three days, three hours, three moments. I turned from rye-bread to jellied flesh to stone & from stone back to flesh.

Born of a stone father, made of baked bread, stoned and grown. Alone in the world as flesh – I walk again.

A walking mollusk now, like the rest of us.

I walk away & Gargoyle Papa looks away, gazing towards a distant rocky planet.

I am free.

I am a soft, decaying human. Which means I have to brush my teeth or you fall over when I exhale. I smell if I don't wash. I blow snot from my left and right nostril and tip my head so boogers will stick to the side of the road & I also have to take a whiz every few hours.

I fart & burp & know the kings & queens & pope and all leaders of those-who-are-being-led do also fart & burp & shit & weep & blow snot daily & have fluids leak from them while they sleep. Even Movie stars pick their noses as I do and flick dried flakes on the floor knowing no one will notice. Sometimes they peel off odd pieces of skin and eat them.

At night, if they're lucky, they come in their sleep.

If they weren't laughing they'd cry. They age & all the bionics in the world cannot avoid the worm feast, the burning smoke, the odd fragment of a forbidden apple that, coughed across a windpipe, makes them choke.

That's me. Human enough to start an office pool about the time of my death.

I'd dance – but there are fresh blisters on my feet.

No need to complain, I think it's a treat to be back again. Bring it on – I'm living the gargoyle's song.

Yep – the lowliest of the low & I like it!

Human.

Inside The Painted Poem Cave:
(Granny Knitwit:
On fire with love & Bread)

There's an apartment in the old purple home that leans towards the sidewalks. This apartment is lived in by our knitting Granny.

Years ago, when the train was steam-hissing to a stop, she wrote her name on a piece of paper & threw it towards a spun cloud.

It rose & then dipped & flew down the street, lifted high again, drifted over the rusty railroad tracks, was scooped up by a raven & became part of her nest. From that point on she didn't need a name. The crows also knew this, and that was good enough for her. Crows knew her name to be *Bao-Bao*. When she was at the end of her skein of yarn, she'd throw it out the always-open window of that old house on Pine Street. Each crow took a turn and scooped the falling wool. Over years the nests tinted multi-colored.

'*Bao-Bao*' screamed nesting babies; '*Bao-Bao*' sang the parents and grandparents.

And she kept knitting, making the crow's music part of the pattern.

In Autumn, her yarn is as scarlet as the maple; as yellow & orange as the birch. In Spring it's green & grey and the first nesting browns, and in summer, the gold of the sun and the full silver of the sliver of the moon hooks yarn after yarn into the scarf of the world.

In winter, her needles tug snow and ice, and glitter dazzles from the endless clicking.

She was left enough money by her mom & dad so she could live her life & pay the rent while following her dream.

Her dream was to turn her room into a salty shrine for Mother Earth - to recreate the Idyllic life of her childhood as it was spent on Salt Spring Island. To knit it inside a book, and hidden-purl the book so it threads yarn through all other books.

She walked all the way to *Kitsilano Home Hardware* & bought paints & canvas & then to *Kearney's Den of Fabrics* & picked out green & gold & blue & purple & orange & brown & black & flowered fabric & begin to change her room into her version of paradise. She dreamed each night of a voice from the Goddess & that voice helped make her room & create the paint-poem-room.

Her hands remembered being a child's hands & painted with innocence & her hands remembered being an old woman who knew the world & those grown-up hands painted the city life; the city world.

One parent (she forgot which) was from Nelson in BC, the other parent (also drifted from memory) was from Corner Brook in Newfoundland. They moved in the fifties to Salt Spring Island. He farmed, she taught. Over the years their faces vanished in her mind, but the gardens were filled with plants from an Aunt Alice.

Now in Vancouver, Granny lives in a house of many rooms, with a garden in the back yard, and a small lawn in the overrun front yard, she kept to herself and knew only that she wanted to leave a room that would remind her of the millennium, where she'd watched one century swing into the other, like an old door with fresh paint. The movement creaked in the same way a door on a celestial hinge might creak.

She stopped oiling the hinges. But she continued to feed the crows. And in the nighttime, when she closed her eyes so she might roam the world, she kept on knitting.

First when she moved to Vancouver, to the purple house, where she had a tiny room & a tiny window, she heard of the small boy in the big room. Sometimes there was a stained tureen in front of his bedroom door. Other times there'd be a full tureen with a green mess of potage. The smell of paint leaked from his room.

His parents vanished, much the same way as her parents were covered in fog and inhaled into a cloud. In her mind, Granny Knitwit believed the house was part of a vast train of time (the Newfie Bullet) & as it swayed through stations of the crossings, it would stop & various people on the train would get off.

She knew each person saw different things when the engine pulled into their waiting station.

A retired Skipper from next door, emerged one January morning. He had on hip waders, and they were tied to his double-clasped belt.

On his head was tilted a fishing hat of many summers, filled with all the flies he'd ever tied in his room. His battered creel, with dried moss peeking out, was slung across his shoulder & he whistled as he snapped the bamboo rod together.

"Why," thought she, "he's leaving the train.

And so he was.

Once, two little girls, hand in hand, dressed in cassocks, headed to school of a spring day. "They're taking the train," she thought. "So young."

And later, when she heard sirens, she knew the train would move on again.

She understood that she needed help. So, she called on the old man who once was a little boy here & he helped her find her new city friends.

Some live in the streets & others live in small rented by-the-day or rented-by-the-week rooms. Some live in ground-nests near rusty tracks. Some pitch near community gardens & help till the soil. Many carry heritage seeds for the day when the world will need to grow true food.

Others show up from nowhere. She believes that some of her friends are beamed down to earth every sunny morning & beamed back home on rainy nights.

Together with the Old Woman, her friends gather poems, they pick sounds, they make the world the way they want the world to be & tho' the room becomes a rainforest room, it also reflects images from stone & city life & discarded clanging hubcaps.

Each of her paintings becomes a grotto-indented shrine. At the foot of some oils are sand boxes with votive candles enclosed in glass with slots so as to catch paper on fire.

Every morning as she awakens, she writes a new poem, even before she puts her teeth in. Every night she burns the poems. She learns how to impregnate the paper with paraffin & later she makes her own paper from old rags, linen tablecloths, shredded. Thrift store paper, is strained & spread in mush over wire from *Home Hardware*.

Sometimes the old man in the big room makes vegetable mush & they spread it thinly over the wire & as it dries, she sees forest faces. She has a battered painter's tray & fills it with water & swirls paint on the surface, and then places white linen paper in it, and it marbles into a dream of Tristram Shandy. She bakes special poems, uses beeswax to impregnate her linen paper & funnels the flames & reads, deep into the night, the age-old stories her long-gone parents had written to her when she was a baby.

She didn't burn these books. Sometimes she sleeps with one or another beneath her pillow.

Her pillow is filled with goose feathers from Fulford Valley farms. She'd made covers from strange fabrics that held her bags of rice. Her head would slip off the pillow suddenly at 3 a.m. but she'd only smile, for she prefers sleeping on slippery surfaces.

She sometimes dreams of rice paddies & of her feet deep to dream-ankles. She hated waking from the dreams. She hopes the train will stop for her near a rice paddy.

In front of each grotto painting, she makes sand paintings of words & images (each left incomplete in one detail.)

She rigs a small oven in the corner. It takes weeks of finding small pieces of metal, old bottles, small broken toy houses, doll's heads, abandoned belt buckles & metal creepers from her very-long-dead-grandmother's boots. Mornings, she adds bottle caps & crows do bring her shiny beads, charms & beach rocks. Afternoons, there's clay from the stream near the airport. All brought from the leaning wall of babies. It takes many bus transfers. Her handbag grows heavy. There are many trips, but it's worth all the back-and-forth.

She loves walking in Vancouver; the way odd smells of cooking float her way from the bushes. She loves being invisible on the sea wall. But more than anything, she loves carrying a purse filled with clay.

Sometimes she feels as if she is clay itself & she moves as slow as Ben-Grimm on soapers; reads comic books as she rides the bus. She cherishes all comix & lifts imprints of her favorite panels & adds them to her shrines.

She doesn't answer the door when people knock. Why would she -?- when she may, instead, play tapes of a Jerry Seinfeld show – the one where Farfel barks.

When the oven's ready she keeps adding things & every night she fires it up. Smoke drifts towards nesting crows click-click-clicking in their sleep, because they know that she's making poem-bread for them. Each night at midnight, she bakes her poems.

Then, click-click-click echo, needles in the night; yarn spins around the world. Once in a scattered while, she knits in a star.

She loves baking with Challah-dough & twisting it into

twirls & curves of words glazing like bakers' showcase breads set on shelves made from biscuit boxes of childhood.

The wood she stains red ochre.

Some poems she keeps for the mice, others she donates to the crows. Each morning they race in & out eating her haikus. She'd peek out to see them do the Long-John-Silver-walking hip & hop around the words.

If she'd written a really good poem they'd fight off sea gulls while they read.

The very old crows memorize some of her best poems. She hears them singing an epic on their way home at night. *Bao-Bao* they'd chant to their offspring. Cluck and clatter. Her words sound just as fine as they tasted.

She walks all the way to Stanley Park in a search for fallen twigs. Gathering special branches, she puts them in an artist's portfolio case. She discovers splinted fragments from the old hollow tree when the wind rips it apart & she brings them home. She glues branches to the walls. The room's made into a forest. There's also driftwood reclaimed, ocean dried & seaweed tangled. Vines & gauze have stick-woven poems of light behind them.

The room is soft. A room of dappled light.

The Sounds?

… Music composed in dreams & learned from her street friends & she finds a CD recorder & music is rendered like barley soup by musicians who have also fallen thru cracks & crashed on the streets where they now play their instruments for pennies. O, think of people with fiddles, accordions, harps & Chinese Violins.

Three old Native People she met while gathering blackberries along the tracks do visit her room & lend their voices & carvings to this place & trees are so thick, that neighbors wonder how a woman may be so silent. They'd have noticed people coming and going from the room, if such visitors had not known how to move with shadows; to leave trees the way bark may release sap. Such visitors may live outside a house and never be heard & may cross a street & not be seen.

Such people became the friends of the Old Woman.

Her door now opens into a forest-swathed entrance that leads in turn to her bread-poem rooms.

One morning the Old Woman wakes up to hear the sound of the train pulling into a new station. A hiss of steam, some squealing of wheels. The voices of two schoolgirls are heard singing a song of their own design & the old woman knows the words as if she'd baked them.

She gets up and washes; naked, her flesh is flapping. She sits for a while in the stream that runs from her sink to her main garden. She likes the way the water follows the paths of her old toes. Remaining naked, the Old Woman slings her purse over her shoulder.

Last night she'd made Challah in the shape of a train engine & she picks up this bread. If a train stops that means it's time to get on. Or 'tis time to get off.

She doesn't look back & carries no keys. She walks out the door; leaves it open. Light washes in the door & she's burned by the intensity. Old stretch-marks gleam. Flesh-folds leak light down her body.

When she blinks, crows spin & hop & sing her poems & she takes a third of the bread & breaks it off & throws the front of the baked train engine to the crows & they caw & cackle & hop around the bread.

The Old Woman smells rice & sees another woman in a long dress & they join together to sing a welcome to the circle of the crows & all schoolgirls join in.

This is another song she's never heard but she also knows those words & sings in morning light & shares the bread as they walk into a new forest almost as good as the one she wrote in her room.

She smiles, knowing she has left the door open.

Seeing her face, you light up when you learn that this is real.

She smiles because you have your shoulder bag ready to carry clay & you know how to bake bread-poems.

There's a vacancy & your rent is free.

The room has been made ready & it's in the house of the small boy in a big room; the home of the naked crone who has left to share her bread with the crow woman. The place where vegetables gossip.

Oh, how sweet is a train of Challah, when it stops at another crossing.

Home - inside the painted poem cave. Down the hall from the retired announcer.

Piano Movies: The sequel/ Flesh Fingers at the keys

Announcer's Voice:

My opinions are nothing more nothing less than trying to make my voice sound like a block of wood.

Announcer's Eyes:

Ah, there's the rub.

His eyes, blue as a Chicago winter, are the only living points in a face that's been around too long.

Across the table sits his wife. As he looks at her smoking cigarettes, one ash falls in the breakfast plate.

Her eyes are rubbed in ashes.

Their eyes are rolled in ash. Smeared across the light are

their eyes. All light is still in that bowl where apples bob on velvet with its skin of night, & all still is light. Their eyes are rubbed.

A hand is made of proton-skin & holds the time when the big boss bounced dice & planets against light that covered laughing night. With the very first bite of that tasty apple, Adam said, "All still is light."

Then he lost all the garden & kissed away the night.

All still is light.

That garden. Kiss away the night, stone lip lock, a grated tongue rasps another. And newly-wound watches marble Adam & Eve.

O...

Bro & Sis...

... that announcer is God. He wrote one of our programs.

That program.

The announcer promised us plenty & got the piano player together with a writer & issued orders & made a big plate for his food. He formed the plate from words and laid it on a screen with the help of meat & music & piano keys & inventors.

Here's what was on the tin plate:

1: Thus was born the screen.

2: Before he worked, he rested & while he worked he rested & when he played - he rested.

3: That boss.

4: You know what bosses like to do when they aren't counting money.

5: His money.

6: Man dollars.

7: He sent out a memo telling Eve & her boyfriend to keep their silence (as they never will or always will) about the night

& the world moving like a serpent's coils, the rattled prattled tail-end of an apple's eye where all the dust is in a whirl & spill & the darkness moves but all still is light.

8: "O, what am I to do? O, what are we to do?"

9: Swallow. Get word-acupuncture.

10: Swallow again, spit out the peel, stamp it into the ground, mix it with mud, stir it with a stick, point words at it.

11: Nail the peel to the wall.

12: Write on it.

13: Write.

And of all the points in the memo, this is the most important one. Tell the boss to piss off. Eat the rest of the apple...

&

then

Write.

Points of light:

Acu-Puncture - This word is a – needle – punching through your skin three inches beneath your navel.

- This word pierces your left leg -

- This word - sticks out from your right knee -

- This word/ digs/ deep/ in your right hand -

/ This word - angles into the skin of your left hand -

- These words/ are nothing. These words are words/ these words are needles – feel - your skin crackle! A pple/ Ap ple/ App le/ APPL E/ A P p l e/ What bites!/ An apple/ a day/ keeps the doctor out of business.

In the country where real winds blow & the smell of flesh is like a ripe apple on the ground there is one small child who is turning towards the typhoon. Here she is – this girl. Right now. Seen on secret satellites – her voice is broadcast to various penthouses which the poor only get to visit if the poor are cooked on platters; apples in mouths.

Printed words blur, lose their grips and sail into word-clouds. They spin and spin and spin around each other.

Here is what the special channel shows:

Grown-ups cling to the trees. They crouch behind shivered husks of cars. Stagger past places where houses are hooked by wind-claws. Birds tumble through the air.

This child - a little girl - is scared until her father rolls across the road and into a ditch. Her mother is fly-swatted to the wall still flicking. O is she scared? No. For the first time since first-breath chills.

The little girl sees what hides behind the wind & her arms go wide as she - for one small second of a year or so - leans on the chest of the wind & her arms go wide as she for that one small second (or a century) sees so well that she lets go of the earth like a dandelion seed lets go of the earth like the Earth releases – a spring and flip – each dandelion seed - like a dot - lets go of a circle.

Now she is flying past the little body that tumbles on the sea. She's turning into flowers that coat the wind with pollen.

She is now the wind.

This girl flies into the words & holds them the way a full-stop holds a sentence.

There are television cameras. They beam pixels to the stars and back again. Eve looks into the camera. The camera lies down, and Eve drifts to & thru the lens.

Chicago-Eyes? He looks at the monitor.

He pauses for commercials.

He and his wife view a tape of what he does. It's called history & they're pretty proud of it. Almost as proud as the inventors of culture.

They're in a Holiday Inn bedroom & there's cable & Bibles open to the back cover & therein is written in the best calligraphy that traveling salesmen can manage:

Why apple?

Why core?

The television says:

…we pause

 …we pause

  …we pause.

"Fox-shit," the announcer thinks –

"What the fuck is this? What the fuck? Who hasn't seen the wind? Big fucking deal. We have snow inside our wind back home. We have real wind."

Suddenly the boss & his wife are in a diner near some sand where limbo-aficionados & random-Mummers dance & television repeats re-runs in the diner.

The special in the diner is about how to cook the flesh of other aliens on the spaceship & it's always the special of the day. Again & again the wind blows on television, disturbing the chefs.

Sand blows past the diner, Barstow sticks in the mind. Sometimes the patterns of sand against the window show animals & flattened humans in scary rooms. Official decrees & proclamations & claws scratching.

That diner.

That storm.

That broadcast.

Restaurant talk rattles round them like cups and saucers. Photos are snapped.

Clouds roll across open eyes.

A dog chases sunset.

A newspaper blows across the boardwalk & you touch my hand. My chest is open; sand blows into my heart. My heart catches each grain of sand and holds it enfolding the touch of your hands on my heart, shaping & fine-sanding it. My heart snaps open-and-closed & spinning-veins are the shutter & you're a Polaroid photograph wrapped around my heart.

A small chair is on the moon. I sit on it and & sing of weeping men. I have a piano, and I play my lunar glass keys while I sing:

Weeping men, with guns, turn teardrops into bullets. Plaid shirts drip red tears until torn hide rests and steams like a forest laundry.

"It's all news," thinks the announcer. It's all news."

Soon the rain cleans the forest, guns are oiled & gleam on gun racks behind locked hearts.

The fire is in the fireplace.

Antlers are nailed inside a photo of a glass of scotch & real hunters in the Arctic do remember women singing into each other's mouths & real hunters in the rain forest are looking at the stars hiding behind the smoke of burning forests.

All through this forest, the sound of weeping bullets mixes with the sound of hawking & the clink of bottles; the cigarette that's buried in its little coffin, the photos - the planes - the private lakes - the cook who knows your name, the guide who calls you by your first name.

The television left on.

(Hey, don't blame me, I'm only the mollusk who plays the piano, writes things down with little mollusk-flanged fingers, floats around. You know – a poet & piano-player.)

Granny Knitwit knits my hands.

Hunters play with an old pack of cards. A cribbage board is near the fireplace. The 29-shaped board is covered with soot from years and years of logs. The stars and galaxies play 29 – that time & those cards & that game. 15-2, 15-4, 15-8. This time.

Hear the sand on the diner window.

Tick. Tick. Tick.

Talk. Talk. Talk.

The forest trembles with the sound of surveillance drones, along with the bite of chain-saws. Whirs & bites.

Men climb cautiously out of planes & stand on docks made from empty oil barrels, where full ones have hand pumps in them & the sound is strangely comforting.

There are no briefcases & this is, somehow, comforting.

There are no criminals to defend or prosecute in court & this is, somehow, comforting.

There are no women at this lodge. Men dream of the olden times of Dick Cheney & his always limp gun. Some hunters shoot hunters.

See Dick shoot. See Dick try to be a big boy.

Men who weep bullets now piss into a lake & hear a loon laugh & think it sounds like boardroom hooting & they tell each other this.

Ferns glow green & glop every channel.

Loons clean ears of sound-tracks, while smoke from late night campfires scrubs teeth of chemo-salsa dip & there are cans that open when you tug the top & there are boots that are impregnated with waterproofing.

Godamn, but Dubbin smells good.

Trees & moss & night & rocks do leaf-cover the engine-like chemical buzz that drones away in late night & makes the ceiling hum until nothing can be done for sleepless hunters, except to create late-nite-TV-infusions steeped in metal and plastic boxes & the hiss of the empty room.

Every time the remote is between channels, the outside

siren calls out names of men.

Later, in plaid shirts and caps, wet with branch tears, steamed by day sky, eyes cooked by autumn, these men hold guns, cry bullets, weep aluminum cookware, pump green camp stoves & stare into campfire flames. They know nothing of hunters in Greenland, who dream golden silhouettes into form, and wide-eyed follow it to the exchange. Their guns are lifted by the moment, and by the dream.

These are not real hunters gathered here. No.

While dreaming of loading their own ammo & tying their own flies, this new bunch will order from quaint catalogs & dream past float-planes & anoint their hands with gun oil.

They smell the oil on stained rag-doll-gun-cleaners & kiss their children good-bye & smell of after-shave all week, but now & forever will smell of rented campfires - these men who aim their tears at deer, at moose, at bears & creatures that fly & at critters that walk on all fours, at beings that have teeth and claws, (such puny teeth and claws rubber teeth and claws) animals of open gut and eyes that will not - oh shit! - will not close.

Gargoyles have no flesh thoughts. We write poems in Hollywood on rock & desert sand, and oil blood beating under the streets. When we see a dead animal we know it's dead. Clik – flesh-switch off.

Look - teeth are sideways in death with the lower jaw angled away from the upper jaw.

Look - they have legs that grow stiff & are unexpectedly blue-yellow inside the carcass.

See - connecting film adhering when outer skin is peeled from inner skin & that membrane is the film that holds the mighty hearts beating in failing boardrooms' near-jumping-CEOs & those veins are surely like the veins that beat in corporate takeovers & those veins are tied around all fingers that remind us guns are aimed at these animals.

O fuck, this is real! This goes all the way back to 2016 real, and 2017 real. When we used to have time and money and opinions. Those days. This is the world I fell into when I stopped being a baby gargoyle.

My feet hurt.

I have to take a dump before I write another word.

Time flows fast enough so here am I back again. I sleep and dream of horses & men & strange landscapes.

I go away.

I'm back again.

I spend a decade in Los Angeles.

I wander round & round for years. Island residents call me elusive.

My skin wrinkles in an eye-blink.

My gut has foundered & my skin hangs loose. Most people I knew when I left the piano behind are now dead.

I get to some funerals on time, I miss most. I have strange new flaps on my body. When I take a piss it takes much longer. Connect the splashed dots on the floor, that's my ever-dying face. Here I am again. That's why most gargoyles climb down just to take a shit, or eat an alien or two.

You know...be human.

Guns are aimed at television & at bad movies. They're aimed at food that tastes like aluminum-foil was used as floss.

Guns are aimed at expense accounts & at nodding to the boss & being too tired too late at night to get it up into the clouds that tickle dicks; dicks that may, sad nights in sad houses, no longer want a dick-tickle.

Guns are aimed at glossy magazines or cars that cost too much. or houses that cost too much & the guns are aimed at bank-machines & house-machines & car-machines & work-machines.

Somewhere, the announcer's hands long for a callous or two.

Somewhere, hands long for just one cut that isn't a paper cut.

And there are hands that want to be broken against the sky & nails that do not have good cuticles & earth that looks coffee-rich on skin & there are minds that want the heft of one good rock. Once in a while there's a thread of white opium in dark hash, sometimes the hash is on a pin. Meditation comes in unlimited forms.

Somewhere, there is something that does not need a gun, yet longs for a forest & a time-wind behind them, a deer in front, a faux-hunter's finger on the trigger, an eye that holds the reflection of the gun-sight along with an animal reflected in the center of the gun-sight of the gun.

They want sharpened sticks, for, when such men can't find bullets to be agents for their tears, they will find a pointy stick & will poke away at living creatures all night. They will study books on arrows; they will grind the edge of hunting knives & they will hone and hold weapons until the weapon is ready to hook an animal in the middle of the eye's world & sticks will plunge when the deer leaps & rocks will fall to crush the deer & an arrow will hide in a deer's flesh & keep wounding while the deer runs & runs & runs until it is in death-burn.

Or, the gun sight will tickle the deer & the man's heart & bile & sweat & the way his itch is all over his body & his teeth taste like 12-gage shot & his eye is open & the deer's eye is open & all the eyes of all the animals of the world are open and looking into our hearts. O, humans, Gargoyles always see what yr up to...

&

animals say to each other:

in that moment between the finger

&

the finger having pulled

&

that moment between the bullet in the gun

&

the bullet in the air

&

in that moment between the bullet in the air

&

the bullet in the outer skin

&

the moment between the bullet in the outer skin

&

the bullet through the skin

&

the bullet in the flesh

&

the bullet exploding in the flesh

&

that moment between being in the forest

&

...in that moment of being on a plate, all the animals say to each other: "Remember when our teeth were sharp & our claws were strong & we could eat these creatures or we could leave them alone?"

&

"O, how they must suffer" say the animals. "How they must suffer, soft men who weep bullets & shoot tears."

Hunters hunted:
The boss speaks – His Wrath:
The Announcer:

Before I knew/ Before I knew/ out /back /the field is open wide/ I looked/ the field is open wide. I opened wide that door/ What I thought/ What I thought was gonna be/ Were other houses/ Other kids like me.

Death, you're like a fucking leaf-blower. /You hit our street, and my pals drift like leaves behind you. You never left a friend for me.

I played.

I played & found my keys & you? Well, you'd gone away into the clouds. The kids & you. So what was I gonna do, except climb inside my piano. What was I gonna do except look for metal in the world?

What is the first song of the boss?

"When the winter is folded in the summer like a taco in my hand. When you are folded like a bullet in the chamber overseas. When I have put the world together one more time.

When I have typed your face.

When I have sung your eyes.

When I have blown you across the sea.

When you've gone.

When I am alone.

When I see the door & open it, I see there's nothing left in the whole wide world except an empty gun hole & me.

When you look at the sky you're shaking gun-shot sparrows into my eyes. Spread across the sky like 12-gage shot. They're leaking down the paper lying on the staff.

When you eat the wires, you can sing the song."

The song is purled on needles of Granny Knitwit.

"What I really hoped (with all my guns) what I really hoped for, was that one day I'd figure out how to build a piano out of them all."

What I really hoped was the family would come round to hear me play.

"What I really hoped was (with the old man in a glass) what I'd really hoped for, was that you in battle-big-muddy-water up to your ass would come to hear my piano?

Walk around to the side, see the little gunports move back. You'd run but you'd run inside. You'd find your own door. You'd open it wide.

You know all this.

Thus endeth another lesson."

O…

…Sing it, my brother & my sister. Deep down you know the truth – it ain't easy stopping being a gargoyle.

Here's the song of the boss. Commie or Capitalist – doesn't much matter. This is what every boss sings in secret sleep… the second song:

"Sparrows. Sparrows, like 12-gage shot hang for a stop-frame moment in the sky. Partridges on the ground. Their necks a question mark?

We're gonna peel the rabbit skin off rabbits, 'cause I think it's growing dark. You talk about your river, you talk about your bombs. You don't know what death and destruction lies in the keys underneath my stony palms.

Someday, if you ever cross me; someday, if you're looking at me, I'll smile - and I'll kill you with my fingers. I'll blow you out the door.

You'll be living with the sparrows - stop frame action in the sky. You'll be there.

Go play away down the river, go juggle with your mines, hold your guts inside your fingers - you're still gonna be feeling fine. Cause it's when you see the sparrows (when you open up the door.)

You're all alone in a house & you know everyone who hears this song can climb inside. Everyone who hears this song can walk away turn around and see the gun."

Hear that –?- yep, the end song of the boss.

Seriously, who really wants to be one?

Not you, I bet.

Not me.

Thus endeth the song of the boss.

My Room has No Curtains

There was the day when it was time for me to find time & finding time, I time-painted away the world of my rooms in the building that creaked its way past (what they called a century ago) memory.

Now is that era when (in the middle of digital surveyors) from one room window there is a condo. (Knit one condo & may as well knit a million.)

From one room window there leans another condo.

I had two blank walls & bugs crawled along those walls. At that time it was the morning & I woke up & I asked the bugs…

- What do I have?

Their answer was clean as my dreams - you have the money that was left by father & by mother.

Not a lot but this pays the rent as long as I stay here. Sounds become my cocoon & so I collect sounds.

I'm taught by what I've left of my childhood from the city where I dreamed of a small Island in the Gulf. I dreamed of growing up. Fucking nightmare.

I will make the island. I have enough money to buy fountains of delight like Kubla Khan in the poem I had read to me when I was a baby Xanadu child. We had little money but we had books.

I asked my friends from the streets to read for me. I folded their voices around me in words I choose.

Oh yes, I bought paints from stores that are filled with shades & wood & fabric & burlap & people who love to talk of color and dreams. And if they can, they'll find just the right shade for those shades who shadow in from the streets, seeking.

When some of us bite the air it grinds teeth sharp and tiny. Noses have slits up the side. Healed, but always cut.

When I lived on the mountain of the island in the ocean & when the light was golden I caught it on the end of my brush. And, oh, I said when I knew this was what I was to do with my life -

- This is a forest-poem cave & will have rocks – I'll get my friends with shopping carts to fetch shattered shale & together we shall build & when it is done, each different room will have a night dream & a day dream to help each room dream & we'll paint the world the way we wish to leave the world!

I shall tell the story of the little boy in a big room. I paint with objects.

That's how I passed the millennium.

And this is the room with no curtains & only a select few shall enter. Those select few shall pass through the rubbish; cross the thin road of exhausted air & leave behind the siren's scream.

And yes, also the delights of the city; the calls of her children; the buzz of many voices talking…

… Oooo, where they go & where they were & where they want to go; the music of asking for a coffee; the delights of the slagging of distant or out-of-earshot friends; the wondering what is around the corner; the stepping off the train & into a lotus (burned by dirty rain but still a lotus.)

The city is where we do not question; where the earth may shake some year or two; where the distant mountains are only sleeping gorillas lost in poems. It's where I once ate Christmas oranges until the juice ran down my sleeve in Granville Island market.

You know the city I describe. Vancouver is the map name.

But the real city has no name, only a sound from the ocean sweeping up the night.

She is the early morning hinge of color…

 She's the sound of moss waiting until buildings are vacated…

She is the name of the deep rooted tree waiting to learn what we will learn.

You know this city.

See her when this room is just a crease in your mind & when you begin to drape and shake, give her your own poem-paint-room – give her your specific name; & when you give this city your name, at that time, by what you say when you speak your poem to this city. You will rebuild that city & all who visit our curving rooms shall see our paradise & she who is in our dreams from when we cried in the alleyway, from when we held our hands out & you walked by shall sing our way past Captain Vancouver – funny-name dude – like Captain Warmart – those names. Now all Captains forever lost at sea; the wrong-way corrugated sons of sons. Thinking he found somewhere that, in truth, by finding - he lost.

Hmmmmm.

New-Name city?

Real-name city?

City of sea-song; smells of cooking; old people gone away to Salt Spring & other Gulf Islands.

Now others who have left empty rooms to seek pain, gather with our kin who have holes in lips, hands outstretched. O we smell of garbage when there's a strike; smell of springtime as soon as February hits.

There are Beaches where we all may live.

I walk into *Home Hardware* and a woman with magical pierces in her ears says "Freak discount! Freak discount!" & gives me & my buddy Sky a discount on the spot. She likes Gargoyle dust.

Empty homes with empty rooms that we may paint. Paint-ball city. City of our heart-beat song. Sea-wall city – smelling of summer fries.

That place.

Go scuttle your ship, Captain Vancouver – we have our place back again as 'tis meant to be. We love her the way a tired sailor loves a hammock. No-name city.

I write from the time before we had merchants try & stop us from asking for money.

Where together we gathered sounds.

Where together we discovered music in shadows.

Where together we built the world as it appeared in our inner eyes.

She will hear our voices -::- know our dreams.

Why?

Oh yes -::- this softness is the softness of your skin.

Oh yes -::- this hardness is the hardness of our bones.

Oh yes -::- this canopy is the canopy of our hair & these fountains are the plash of our blood.

Remember when you saw me first, Old Lady?

Near the corner of your eyes I was gathering shadows. Near the edge of your rear view mirror, I was picking up poem words.

With my buckled hands I was humming my songs & trying out my poems for the ears of the wind.

Leave the city and see Her. Stay in the city and she's there.

Remember the revolution of 2018 when we threw out the money-laundry-relators and those with dirty money? Trump was gone & we hung thousand-dollar bills on clothes-lines so birds could have them for their nests, and all at once, the crows sang *Bao-Bao* in happy celebration?

Remember when we had places for us all?

I have, with my friends, painted a shrine for the revolution.

Before I died.

But it has only one lodging place.

Now that I am gone; It needs the lodging place of your heart.

It needs the blood beat of your own drum blood.

It needs the eye light of your glimmer-catching-orbs.

It needs the true life web site of your spider-thoughts.

It needs you.

Help spin me past the century door & bring the

forest to each stained room.

Carry your heart in your hands.

And we may all kneel towards you to hear it beat.

Go forth and help re-charm the world (Your eyes, ears, flesh, and heart open)

And a new wind shall blow into each new-born room; taking away the angles & circling with your circled life, this world; this wren of a morning world; this moss soft smell of a ripe & green world.

&

She will see you plant

&

She will grow crystals in the sweet Mango morning

&

In the deep green rain forest of our veins

&

In the bone-cave-hollow of our heads, where eagles perch until we fly.

Feel. Touch. Taste. Sing the song that only you may ever know.

I was old & I had to go away. Before I did, I left for you (my stranger) (my friend) this Poem-Painted Room.

Pick up yr brush

&

Paint now – O - Sample the delight of an empty room.

My room has no curtains.

A trine forms:

Newfoundland trines Vancouver & trines Hollywood

Knit/
unravel/

knit again.

Where I live after becoming mollusk-human:

White with square folds pressed in by the packers at Montreal, catalogue girls are skipping with yellow skipping ropes.

Skip – Slap – Skip – Slap – Skip – Slap.

Tidy is their skipping & their new clothes do crinkle through the prairie winds sending the boys' Roy Rogers shirt fringes a-dancing; wooden guns are smoothly aimed.

Round & round the whitewashed rocks steps are drawn. They dance with my sister, spirit of Bonfire Night.

The bell stops its clapping. Like tissues they all drift into the classroom.

See the wandering poet? Once he was a student at the school; years ago he wore a white hat.

Now, he's a forgotten Grandfather, rocking slowly to and fro.

Sometimes his chair skids sideways on the ice that's forming thick & low upon our raft. His piano is on another raft. Grandfather Gargoyle.

He doesn't care, just rocking in the chair as ice candles burn along the edge of his newspaper.

The radio makes its own blue haze, forming a thin wedge of sound against the ice that glazes TV in a glaze of ice so all the sound spills ice cubes on the wood.

The waterfall holds a turn that lifts the old man from our raft & holds him in a hand of ice that tosses him the way only a mother could toss, into the spray-filled air, where he takes a tumble & a spin & settles in his chair perched upon a cloud.

Singing loud, bouncing like a hi-toss ball, this Grandpa (cloud & chair together) takes a turn around the air & then there's nothing there!

Who am I?

I am the child of the child of the child of the gargoyle. As I age, I become my own child.

My bones tell me this. My nails tell me this. My teeth tell me this, my gum sockets tell me this. I am mineral as much as animal as much as vegetable. Mow my hair & it grows back.

No big deal. I'm the Chia-Pet poet.

The deal's enough for me. Go ahead, mow my hair, makes my skull itch. I like it. I smile.

Even grandfather gurgles into fish-life with a smile on his kisser.

Where you stand and feel the autumn wind leafing up your hair & dusting your mind, my aunt once picked the red currants all a-burst upon her finger tips.

My uncle stirred the barking kettle and dipped the twine while I wooden hammered oakum hammered wooden oakum stroke/ built/ stroke.

I hammered (oakum hammered). See. Hammered, the ribs hold beach rocks now, hammered sense into our heads/ our aunt did - strap flying through the air.

Leather taste split the air./ Welts. Lying in our bed (burned to the feathers) pillow-teared to the eye. Taste of flannel hot on bed sheets.

Hammered the fence post till the paint shook off & the driftwood/ split quivers across the pickets & moss is near hay.

A foot path

w

   i

     n

  d

s

thru the kitchen, until the hammer has no handle & the steel grows in winds-and-crooks of a boy's own tree-arm held knotted. Near knuckled horseshoe & pursed nail, a lone lover's knot twists a little.

Lean over the frankum across the opal & bite into a pitch-blend-crumble.

Teeth stick.

You sniff and smell the air that blows over the barking pot & past the popped kelp blisters in moist pot liquor; licking the striped gooseberry & seeing (in a haze) the stripe shimmering stone walls & feel night's tongue shiver & pop the dark bubbles in the walls.

The path now curls downward through the kitchen & oakum is mouse-nested into warmth.

The hammering has stopped, lights are buried in the meadow. All the sounds (the wisp, the rush, the crack & stillness of your picnic blanket leaping in the autumn air) echo in all the sights. Our hair a-dust, a leaf joins hair, joins dust in the autumn wind.

Dust drifts over railway tracks & rusts.

My lady walks through the wide field by the railway

station.

Her white dress is stretched by the wind &, catching on the brambles; shimmers & grows a child to hide behind her. She is here to call on us. Above the grass, below the grass, inside a rock, outside a rock – a rock itself, a sand-being, formed by fungus on a stump, patterned into life on a leaf, She sees us all. She may melt stone. She may melt flesh.

The 'Newfie Bullet' has the old steam engine, and smoke makes clouds. That train stops where the tracks have died & melted in the sun. It rests in purple grass. It tilts, leaning like a snake.

The porter and a salesman stop the argument they were having in the smoker & blow their own smoke out the window.

There's a stream & in the stream there drifts a Gargoyle Grandfather in his rocker; off his rocker; down the stream; around the bend. Yeah.

A schoolgirl choir is walking on the grass.

Snaking on the hill, each bend holds a white-socked cassocked singing girl.

They sing her into this world. Their voices hold no aliens. Just us. No fuss. Just us. A bunch of animals, vegetables, minerals. You know, sentient beings. Yep – all of us.

Granny Knitwit knits an ocean & swims in it.

With each stroke she grows older; with every wave she grows younger. At twenty-five centuries, she's young again. She is in an ocean of wool, and it curls into combers. She is in an ocean of purple lichen dye. It is a forgotten loom & then it starts again, and knits Granny herself into the warp & woof & rolls her in rollags of golden yarn to lie on the beach the way shavings are on a 1900 workshop floor.

The dust becomes dust-drops & she Knits/ Knits/ Knits.

Swimming, at twenty five centuries in currents from a distant shore, sand fills the water turbo-charged, silting, shifting pebbles nearing gargle, rush, spits.

Sand melts light, folds a star frappe; melts more light

to surprise and lift the swimmer's plumes;

  the wake of pixilated water

    the sounding of the depths by dolphins

     the permeability of it all.

This is new

   this lifts

    this lands

     this swims.

new

found

land

where I was ground

B

C

where I

am ground.

The digital domain is just another filter; (mathematical filter)
trying to strain, in whirling filters, the sheer grind of the world
where nothing goes away; not even what has left.

   We swim in pyramids

   King Tut has gauze:

   unravels beneath a transparent

   jellyfish.

We swim in particles,
old whales, cows, guns
netted by deconstructed matter.
Galaxies are carried
by the ocean
as are we
as are you.
The stars float to the bottom;
slide along our angled cutting arms
in deep Seas.

From a nearing beach
lights a-pulse,
pulse-thumping light
against our chests
all of us swimming
together, tho' apart
all in an ocean with no name.

Stars ride the chariot of the world
or are just
stars
before they're named.

What is
            is real

What was

       is real.

Each age leaves behind
its sand, its striated stars
we swim with Cortez
who breathes
the sound of different voices.

We swim, our capes behind us
like those worn by witches
knit
in Norse sagas
       light-capes, star cloaks.

Our sand follows us,
phosphorescent,
aglow with transmogrified oceans.

At twenty-five we feel the water
At twenty-five we let our toes sink
and find the ledge
feel
beneath our
feet
a particulate ocean.

The beach approaches
you
approach the beach
& above the dunes
is glimpsed
    a surprise
        the moon held
            in the ocean
                of the sky.

Twenty-five centuries
    the ledge that
        lifts our feet

as we stand
    Terra Nova
        approaching.

As we swim
    Hollywood
    approaching.

The Road/The Horses/
The Dogs of A Strange Town

On my first journey along the road to Hollywood, I was about to grab a tree to help me climb the cliff when I noticed, near the base, a weakness as it leaned & broke away from me & fell in one second a thousand times, lifting dust and needles, blowing in a brown and green cloud past the woman holding a baby in her arms with a child clinging.

This is what it is to stop being a gargoyle.

Her hair was blue wool knitted into rows. She was the wife of a man who'd left the school and gone to live in some small outport.

This blue-knit woman was hanging on to my every word & asking about the city while I stroked her hair as the children watched. She'd told of how her husband owned a store he'd built behind a square white house. They'd seen pictures on TV of the gargoyle who became a poet. They'd heard the story. Read the poems on a blog in India. 'Caught up with the news.'

Hey.

She wondered how his hair would feel if stroked by her fingers. Now she gets to find out.

In that store, an oval mirror was half-hidden by a white-and-yellow-haired old woman in a floured slip that could be cooked and baked & would turn out crisp & true from any wayward oven & kitchen. Flour was also on her hands.

The more I looked at her hair, the more the yellow showed – like the bounce off a winter's sky. She smelled of lemon juice.

The old woman and I nodded hello through the upper curving of the glass & asked each other how the kids were; how, indeed, they were during the each-&-every-day.

"O," she said," they are now growing grandchildren; behind my back they grow them!"

BTW - added she - if when you send no gifts because yr broke, they break them away, and call it good.

I thought this was so stupid, I took it as a joke.

Then it was no joke, for those who stop thinking with the heart go to the hard-place where rocks are tumbled in the head like reverse gem-makers, turning diamonds into coal. What pretty coal. Such pretty coal. Where can we sell it?

When I learned this truth, I cried so much that tears fell from my nose to the beach, and dogs grew with every tear.

I looked out the window where the waves hit, before the sound could reach the room.

To the right, were cliffs that, 45-degreed-straightened to hold houses with the colors licked off and roofs bitten and crow-legged walking to cross the boil-holes where foam rainbowed the windows.

"I lives there," said an old woman.

"Do the waves reach?"

"Only sixty feet high, sir."

"Do you get scared?"

"The horses might kill me but they haven't yet & I been there eighty years."

To the left it was calm.

In the middle beach, long coat-hangers of horses were walking & had dead dark-n'-light hair-manes/ were slinkies in movement/ slinky-springs to the side stretching & flowing/ they curl/ they whip into seventy foot high waves of motion/ o, claws of broken watch springs/ teeth of halved razor blades.

O, moving (all stilts-to-the-wind) / next / are the dogs of a strange town.

And then again the horses. The beach pounded fountains of silicon in the air hanging in goblets the horses stamped windows in the beach broke them & candy crystal was their munching of people.

Hey, there's new aliens in town.

Little ones, white and tubular; tippy on tiny legs.

And here come the horses!

Ribbed steam boilers.

Factory chimneys.

Wrapped in white spun glass, their mouths have blue lips & those manes. All dried into sea weed, tangles in bone - blood rusted. They stamp the dogs into the sand beneath their hooves.

I want to go home.

"Easy," they all said. "Easy, just keep going past the beach. Find the missing piano-island."

I looked out the window at a nearby drop of earth where a horse bit a tiny man by the head and lifted him all a-dangle till his trunk plucked loose and did the red-and-white against the rocks.

The horse spat at a fence and splintered (all red-and-white) the gate.

I rushed to the door to find the town was coming to see me.

The first in line was driving a cart with the huge horse in traces.

He rode it towards me and each stove-in board ribbed my back; drove me against my spine.

I laughed and nodded to prove it was, by nature, a joke, like turnip babies & the heat of the horse steamed past my ears as the fisherman left his cart & said, "No more than you deserve" & strode towards the store.

The others smile and watch as now I am slammed again & again against the building – now red is on the white.

No gargoyle, I am human. I bleed. I could die again.

Tilting over them in a lost rising moment, I (the earth a-spin) am worried by the teeth; relax & am shaken into the bite, the red and white against the sky.

Still-points made of rocks speak to each other in sand-words, rock-words, silica-circle-words; the corners hold no corners; circles circle.

See?

Life was a piece of cake. Make no mistake about that. We thought it was caught & held, a ball in blue and brown, rolling down, an easy catch for you and me.

I fall – I rise, I drop on & then into the earth.

The sand slams me into stone.

Stone home.

Dead flesh. Soft.

New Journeys/Old Journey:

On my final journey along the road, the two men seem neighbors.

One is called George & he complains to the driver about wild dogs & wonders why the city council can't find a way to leash those red-&-white biting dogs; a way to chain them from the prowls of night.

The driver says how only last week the final postman floated thru their teeth.

His letters are written in red and white.

All the talk has covered the squeak of brakes; the rasp of disk, the shush of tires against the sidewalk.

Old men looking in the window have their raincoats slicked down by the rain.

Cars flatten rain. The corner window of this corner house is splashing trees & is oiling leaves.

Boards are creaking while the needle-&-pump men laugh their way towards the room.

My veins are ready to tickle to the joke.

My arm breaks upwards & the echo tings. A galvanized funnel's echo is whispered through the dull orange hose.

A gray twig caught by the trunk of a green tree pokes into

the shadow cast on the pool. One leaf floats first into then out of the shadow.

Wind-drops cling to a spider's web. The web is spread between a tree planted last century & one planted in the Eighteenth century where, for a while, it seemed all the answers had arrived.

A moment must have come when all poets sighed & knew they weren't alone; knew the creeping worm might somehow swallow other points of light, but printing made the books escape the worm's turning as we cast pounds and pence against the darkness.

This is how I think when I am dead. Lots of time to think. Next incarnation I intend to meditate on Hume.

Lace the handkerchief & carve a chair into the copy of a form.

See dust drift off a pyramid & see the Nile scrape weeds & trickle into the sand.

Turn.

The worm turns & dust rolls down a pyramid. We watch money cast at the night. Warp and fold through time, returning as a house, or as cars, as turnpikes are walled against the drifting dust of sand that dusts the coast worms its way into the meadows.

O, I am dying – and floating thru the 18th century.

If I were alive now it would be a puzzle. When I died, the puzzles changed; became odd somehow.

And then simple.

Look at the dust and read in it, the eighteenth century.

I float from there to hear an Inuit poem, chanted in the darkness. See the seventy-odd words for snow still fail to keep it far away.

Deny the melting of an ice pan as I tattoo my song on you.

Dip my song in blood upon the snow. Dive on an iceberg from my Hindenburg, let my words roll in the ocean & ride the horse across your enchanted skin.

Swim the moat & dive into a molecule.

Write every book.

Sing all the songs.

And, as you sing all the songs, even the ones we thought were hidden & I drift across the face of the houses of the house of all worms, see the pyramids, breathe me in & cast your body against the darkness. That's enough for me. Drink these words thru a straw. Have a piss. Write a book.

See this as a point of light until you join me in the molecule's roll until you drift across the sand until you & I are sand.

Before we get up - the bed is warm and holds the imprints of our bodies, footprints deep and dusty.

After we get up, the bed cools and flattens & there's no sign anyone ever slept there. There is no sign we were ever there.

The wind blows sand. The bed stays cool. A distant dog does bark.

And the moon goes full.

I die and turn to wool, caught by needles, tugged into stone shape...again.

Granny Knitwit finds the perfect fit:

The kitting is with needles made of smoke, thru the walls, into a cave, knitting smoke to smoke; world to world.

Time for birth. Time for math.

Wane & wax.

After math:

A baby's head is burning. Wax white candle.
A clock ticks once or twice before its spring runs down.

The baby is swaddled in wax clothing. White wax is melting from the baby's head. The room is still, except for the sound of a candle dripping on marble. Grandfather's chair tips as he goes over another waterfall & into the pool that spreads into the sand & down into the hole in the earth and spins, spins, spins.

Blip.

Once you were little & had no one to protect you except a family. Poor you.

Once you looked up to see the flowers.

Once you were lost inside a parent's eyes; a parent's hands - a favorite aunt or uncle or neighbor, sister or a brother, neighbor, clergyman. Their big eyes & their big hands were all the better to eat you with & tear you with. If you weren't one of the lucky ones who left alone was never alone...

... if you weren't, you were tugged into the secret place, lost inside the grownup's secrets. That place where they took you places no child should have to go & (fingers on the lips) had nowhere else to go except to at evening's close - when another little child, a dumpling piano baby - asks you to stay where you & he are safe: ah, that's the scary ticket.

Stay and play inside my piano & take my hand & spring on strings inside the piano & skip and jump in a place where there are no secrets.

We know the serpent was a smokescreen, we know that all who hurt others, always say, "We must keep this secret."

No. This is a place where all the secrets have been let out and only music stays...

...We play across discarded skins of flying-saucers of dreams.

Lights spin across the surface.

One video camera-projector searches for faces. Faces spin across the flying saucer.

The music is wide enough & deep enough & true enough to be our playground.

Little girl, little boy, come and play in the piano playground where there'll be no secrets.

We are children rolling down the wires & dancing on the keyboards of our piano playground.

Come with us to the planet of Piano Island.

The words echo & strobe & the saucer flies & the metallic shell goes back.

Now on its face we see painted piano-rolls of philosophers & piano players & plumbers & engineers & crooks & cops & various deadbeats & heroes & people who would do a three-finger-barf if they saw a hero-poet & the color is sky blue & the music & voice concludes & the sound of spheres rings out the arrangement of space/ of life - between the void/ the stars.

I creak. My stone eyes open. Quartz fingers. Flesh gone. Gargoyle once more.

On the edge of the roof, I am perched. I have a marble piano. Gargoyle Father, Gargoyle Mother clear their throats & dust drifts from our mouths into a new world.

Father wants to sing a valley. Mother wants to sing a volcano.

In Harmony we wish to sing a star or two.

We don't care much about time, for we have none.

We start with space Mobius-stripped thru the blind spot of each eye.

Stone-ripples. I sound the first chord.

Together we sing

you

&

me

stone

deaf

ears open

or listen

in silence. Gargoyle poets have a lot to say…because we embrace thoughts behind thoughts behind thoughts. Hands on chins we eat the clouds.

I am carried to the past future to see my selves.

I have no idea who carries me; sometimes I see my life, sometimes I see only those who see me. This time, I'm placed in a Museum. The place is called Vancouver.

Of a Monday morning is when it happens. Granny Knitwit sees me. I see her. She walks up to me.

"We've been waiting. It was the dogs again, right?

She knows for sure when I nod. "I need to get the others, there's been two floods, a city flood and a time-flood. Things mix together. More of you on the move. More of me on the move."

Deep night I hear a song from the big old house. That's how I know I'll be leaving the museum of culture, going to my true home. I'm meant to live where rocks & people talk & all moons & suns & worlds are heard.

That place.

I hear an old familiar voice. A friend…

Singing Underwater

(The Boy & Girl in A Bigger Room)

Before I married the small boy in a big room, I lived in my own. I was known as the big girl in the small room of the house that was big till it was torn down & even then it kept right on going, like the phantom skater of Boulder, so, perhaps it was inevitable that we'd get together.

Long ago, when there was air & earth & sun & touch, I sometimes bathed in water, drank it, filled water balloons with it & leaning out my window, dropped the slo-stretching globules watching them stretch thru time & compress space.

That was when the little boy from the next floor rode his green bicycle. Slower than the old Newfie Bullet. A stopped train.

He'd look at me and laugh – water over his epaulettes & even tho' he wasn't allowed to play with other people, I knew he was my best friend.

Once I hit him right on his little helmet & the spike burst the balloon, spraying it over his shoulders. He rode round and around, with scraps of balloon fluttering from his helmet. He screamed aloud that he would marry me & years later outside Barstow, on our way to Lone Pine, we did marry. But that's another story for another day; another life.

What I must tell, what I will spill over these pages is so filled... so spilling, so warm that we could take a million nights and fill a trillion fishbowls, so we might swim together.

My feet are submerged. Ever since they boarded my door shut & the taps came on, my feet have been wet.

I ruin more shoes this way.

Once upon a time, my Aunt Irene, who (once upon another time) was placed in a larger fish bowl (in a much bigger room) & made the mistake of wearing red shoes & her shoes were, let's face it, not of their original color which was white, a white that scuffed and shifted through the roads that Aunt Irene walked & bulged because of the pressure of her corns and bunions. The white shoes were so scuffed & corn-poked that one day she decided to color her life with red shoes.

Little did she know she'd be wearing red shoes for the first time with the skim of new dye of new vermillion holding & bending color around her battered feet on the same day that she'd be placed in a fish bowl.

No one told her she'd be in a fish bowl.

No official sent a message. The Queen didn't send a telegram. The Pope had no fishbowl-day-chant-along-gram.

And now here am I, door boarded shut, waking up each morning in a slowly-filling-up-with-filtered-water fishbowl.

I was trained never to complain, so I make the best of it. I squeegee the sides of the bowl & fill a bucket.

When I need to go to the bathroom I use a bucket hanging from a broom which I've notched. I've fitted the bucket handle into the slot that I'd chewed into the end of the broom. I raised it to the edge of the fishbowl & tipped it down the side.

The room is starting to look – well, pretty terrible, but I'm lucky to have the fishbowl to protect me.

I'm not one to complain, so I don't – not even when the skin on my feet grows white and puffy. I peel off old skin, and place fragments in the slop bucket & think to myself that things could be worse & there are children all over the world in much worse circumstances.

I don't know any such children, but have faith that they exist. I pray for them every night. The fishbowl gives a lovely echo to my words, so I pray aloud, just to hear the ringing of my voice.

I sleep on the coffee table in my fishbowl. Lately it bobs around, for each night (no surprise) the water grows higher. I have a fishbowl on the coffee table in my fishbowl. It has another fishbowl on the coffee table inside that. Beyond that my eyes don't go. Too many fishbowls.

It was just after taking a long drink of water that I noticed I was in a filling fishbowl. I'd tried to pour more from the carafe – but it was unexpectedly empty. I was so surprised that I dropped the carafe into the rising water, where it still bobs.

Once in a while, I dip up a glass of water from the bottom of my bowl & drink slowly. I know my feet have been in the water a long time, but no one's perfect. Water-sogged skin-curls in a carafe are small prices to pay for being alive.

Remember this: you're never told when it may happen to you, when your ankles will flood; when a bursting baby boy or girl of womb water will gush from beneath & make your gut a miraculous spring. Sometimes babies are lost in the flood. Sometimes, the flood leaves babies behind. Sometime ankles feel water rising, past the ankles. More times it gushes thru the body all at once. Right to the feet.

When it happened to Aunt Irene, she knew only that she had new shoes & that she could follow her feet to happiness. She let her nylons grow firm & muscular, felt them clasp her thighs, let her thighs flash a whiteness that, albino-ivy-sped-up-film style, glistened up her belly, upwards over her breasts, whitewashing her throat & finally coating her face & making her look like a Noh-play sweetie.

But that day; that day of Aunt Irene (like my day this day) became for her a fish-bowl day. It was, as is this, a day of bend-the-light-with-glass & put a woman into warm languid water. From her days as an acrobat, she was able to handspring, bracing her feet against the side of the bowl, upside down, so her red shoes wouldn't grow wet.

I couldn't do that, because my shoulders are weak & I still use lung-breath. Even stone lungs need air.

Aunt Irene felt her hair soak as it trailed in the water. She felt her skirt slip-slide downwards until it bunched around her waist. But she didn't care - for her shoes would carry her through; would draw eyes from those special places where eyes (even in the mind) shouldn't be, over to the tight bunching of red shoes.

Until the water reached her eyes, she had to look at all those gathered around & who were eye-balling her through the open door. She observed them from her upside-down position under water. Her fish bowl had in front, her mother, trying to hide her daughter behind an apron & her father, who smoked a pipe and read a paper & there were her lovers, who strolled around the bowl and discussed what they had cherished about her & the doctor who delivered her first still-born baby; all of them were fish bowl watching.

And she knew she would drown – not because of the water (she knew how to breathe through the emerging gill slits in her throat) but because she knew those staring eyes would let her sing in their eyesight.

Bending down, she loosened her shoes & released them. By now the water had reached her waist.

With nothing to lose, she began singing. She gargled her favorite song that she'd learned at a High-school reunion in St. John's. She got around. Even for her birth, she got around.

…*I'm living on the moon. Beams hold me in their arms. Since you moved away, I swear I'm here to stay. I'm living on the moon. Moondust inside my heart. Earth floating in the sky. Bought a cape of stars. Hope I haven't gone too far.*

I'm living on the moon. The moon is in your eyes. Sliding down your spine. When the stars shine, it might cross your mind. I'm living on the moon. Come here & join me now. Please listen to me sing. Close your eyes and try, to softly cry my name.

We float inside the moon. Twisted shadows in your room.

We're living on the moon.

What Aunt Irene should have done was remain upside down & breathed in the water. That's what I'd have done. But, I'm no acrobat, I'm only a mother.

My water (like Aunt Irene's) is warm. As it sucks at my calves, it is very, very warm.

When I was little, I stayed at Aunt Irene's house at the time she still had white shoes (shoes that were scuffed and bunion pushed.) I wet the bed. The bed had flannel sheets & I was awash for one happy moment in warm piss & snug flannel sheets. Snuggling deeper, I kept peeing until I was empty & the bed full. That one moment was a toast-on-the-hands-butter-&-crumb moment; the way this water feels now, except that it doesn't chill afterwards. It doesn't need to be scrubbed; it is not hang-the-sheets-in-the-night-time & wait for them to dry.

Aunt Irene flipped back to her feet & her new red shoes went under water & in only seconds the crimson dye was in the water. Snaking scarlet to the top of the water, it smoked red flare smoke into the womb-warm wet cling of the water & that was what had embarrassed her - not her underpants at the top of her, not the curved ascent of her legs, but precognition of red water.

The flow made her flip back & stay in the water until all that was left above the surface was her Noh-face. Her chalk-white face above the red water - O, an egg on scarlet. Her body vanished in a plume of water & no person said one word. All day she stood taller and taller; just her head above the magic red water.

I wondered: could she have breathed in the water; could she have sucked it in? An aqua lung is no good. With an aqua lung you must breathe in & out & never hold your breath. Each breath must not be forced out, nor each breath willed in. If you panic & hold your breath & rise only four meters, you will Uncle-Bert your way to death.

Uncle Bert was Aunt Irene's husband.

The day she dyed her shoes, the day the dye turned her feet red, that was the same day Uncle Bert told me he was magic.

The night after I wet the bed he visited. "I'm magic," he said, "I have a magic snake. It will never bite, it may only spit."

That was the day that Aunt Irene dyed her magic red shoes; the night when she came into the bedroom to see what she never knew she'd see.

My aunt was in bare feet; a nightgown & bare feet. I was crying and saw that her feet were red & she ran across the room & hand-slapped Uncle Bert (slapped him hard) & he left & she stayed & the water was all around me when she held me.

Can I learn to breathe water?

Uncle Bert couldn't. He took his Scuba gear & he dove deep & he held his breath & then he kicked. Without his tanks, he quickly rose to the surface, where his lungs blew out. When they exploded, he was filled with red water, it spilled from his mouth like a red scarf. It beet-juice-foamed in a red-crested wave.

He is no longer magic, yet he swims beneath the waves.

Aunt Irene is magic & she swims inside red waves.

My shoes are white, my heart is pale & I swore I would never love a man, but I did. A man who loved the smell of ripe peaches & liked the way I looked any time of the day or night. I swore I would never find myself in water warm & rising like blood-tide - but I have.

I swore that I would not think of water, that I would live in the heart of the Mojave & I did. I swore that I'd only drink water from tinfoil survival packs. That I would snip the corners with small nail scissors & I would suck in the water with my eyes closed & I did & I sailed them outside the house & just like when I lived where I used to live when I was not a widow & when I had two boys & when I had a husband who wooed me by the way he ate a peach (who would lie on top of the skin of the ocean like all water was the dead sea) & swore if I didn't like waves the way they were, he would paint them for me.

He would bring me white water, orange water; water painted a deep Aunt-Irene shade of red.

I lived near Lone Pine, and put a blotter-paper host on my tongue.

We left the desert and lived near fences.

We lived near peach trees.

Another time, we lived near the beach by the ocean & now the beach is in my heart. That's what I'm to tell you. That & magic & when I mourned all that I mourned I mourned from the sluices of my heart & I mourned the way water went red & I mourned the way Aunt Irene never used her trapeze again; how it was curled up to the rafters & never let down.

I have attended a year of funerals. I've walked on desert dirt & now I'm in the fishbowl. I understand that gargoyle children do not drown.

My sweetheart, when he left his room, when he got off his bicycle – when he ran on land with me, made only one big mistake. Instead of living near Lone Pine, instead of growing cacti & reading the collected works of Franklin Merrell-Wolff, we came back to the big house.

In the desert, people don't drown in magic shows, the snake may not drown them, the waves that dissolve sugar-hair may not melt them.

All children, like water babies, know how to breath under water. I do not know how many people I've told this to. As many people as did not listen - that is how many children I have told this to; as many children as float near Laguna Beach; as body surf the rip-tides of Zuma.

Aunt Irene should not have hand-flipped.

Uncle Bert was right to breathe his own blood.

And babies always hide in the current. Mud-smeared they spin like hydro propellers.

The water was over Auntie's head, but she breathed.

The little boy from the big room drowned in air. Different from children who were dragged into a wall of mud.

I saw him there, on his bed, sucking in the air that drowned him. I heard gargles & gurgles & with a smile on his face saw how he strangled in air.

Now the water is close, now, I am magic.

Now I am no child's mother, no man's wife.

The fishbowl is filling. All have gathered to pick over my belongings.

I am nobody's anyone.

I am magic.

I am the underwater swimmer.

Please tip the fishbowl over when I drown & please comb my hair with waves & please - drown me in words & song.

Like Aunt Irene, she is breathing water.

I am fish bowl happy - nowhere near dry caskets.

The water is a bubble & we float.

We float.

Stone Rafts

Gargoyle Baby Poets stretch each bubble. Milk-pod froth, bee's-eye view, house-fly vision, the ocean fills with baby Gargoyles. Bubbles' stretching skins roll us all towards Zuma Beach. Surfers smile as all the me that there can be, does roll in different faces, am typing with baby fingers ashore.

"Dude welcome to Zuma" says one & the one is me.

Always best to write yr own death poem while you can, especially if already dead.

Yeah, peeping out past the Gargoyle mask, is me. Typing in stone in the museum of my now dead mother.

"Dude?"

Shades are round, face is a grin, his hat aimed at the sky. Beneath the fingers, the standard-issue gargoyle typewriter - mica waiting for my slate-keys to keep a slamming.

Shades lifted, his eyes project me in twin beams of light, Roman-Kroitered across the 70mm sky.

My eyes meet my baby eyes, and all I write, the outports that I dream, the homes, the paths that trail their way along the cliffs are spliced to the ghost town that awaits me when I wake or when I sleep; the hand that will knock at any door, goes thru all my life, past knives being sharpened in Rome, and late night Opera Singers, with wheels around their necks, past the lower, and upper Battery, down Forest Road, on Burgeo Ice pans, in Bonne Bay lugging a projector across the ice with Charlie Reid, falling down a cliff in Gros Morne, past the marriages, & all the unseen caskets of melting friends, pumiced in Pele's hands, rolled in beads of salty quartz, past Ganges.

And there – behind it all is me, the tiny poet, typing his way into mud banks and out.

Dead gargoyles write a lot. And make a tree look like a mayfly.

Joined by my dead father and my dead mother, I leave my disguise far behind. Discarded gargoyles that I wrote do sink to form a new reef for Zuma. And sharks swear on my very name. It is time to write the lodestone truth. I am in my dead mother's empty condo & my eyes are yarning knitting-needle out, bubbles bursting, yet instead of sinking...

I

am

to

float inside the river

of

my

opening eyes.

The Gargoyle Ascends:

Oak Moon

&

Storm Moon

I am dying, as I write this story; as this story is written, I am having a break down; breaking down, I am falling in small pieces of ink and paper. I am falling snow through a black sky; flakes upon my shoulders.

Chaste Moon:

The moon in Vermont is clear cold light; is draped across my arm, I am carrying a blanket to cover lost babies & it shimmers, a clear mantle on my arm.

I'm so far from home.

I hear the trees. Is there a missing baby!? A boy? A girl? Can we help?

Before I left Los Angeles, the bed was warm, it held the imprint of my body in warm sand & crooked footprints stayed there like crushed cigarette butts in ashtrays outside delivery rooms.

My footsteps leave the bed.

The bed stays cool and my body is ready for the city though this body is not a baby body not a newborn open to the universe not a boy-body ready for the Plainsfield forest brave & barefoot in the snow. I'm willing to leave blood prints on the snow to track down baby voices. In the bathroom the mirror shimmers edges green and neon. My face is caught between reflection & a forest.

We are made of meat and music. We are born with sawdust on our feet. We are glued to our mothers for a while. We fall into the angles of our father's eyes. And they look anywhere but where we are.

In the forest the songs at first are faint.

What babies are these? I wonder, because I have heard their songs.

I'm a little boy & know I should ask my parents before approaching the forest. But before my parents can awaken, although it is winter & the wood has swollen & wood is plimmed against wood, I push the window so the grain squeals, I'm squeezing myself even smaller & push & push & push through the narrow opening.

I hear dead babies singing - their words as clear as eyes.

Glued to our mothers for a while, we look into our brother's eyes & out the other side. Breezes are cold, and no one told us that we are made of meat and music.

As I walk towards the forest, the voices push before me. I start to run. The night is cool & snow's on the ground & I'm in bare feet.

Seed Moon

*C*old days on the moon we smile & for a while you may see us; *sawdust on our feet - moondust blowing through our hair. We are the stars beneath your fingernails, but you must dig deep. We may be reflected in your eyes, But you must look down the deep well. Yes, you must look down the deep well.*

Our eyes spill night time. Please, oh please scoop stars from the shadows. Our fingers move like fallen stars - say the babies to me - dip inside your eyes. Find... your body.

Hare Moon

*F*riends fall away like fireworks on a deep night in Vancouver. At first, years ago, when friends were there for no reason, I had no answer when I was asked: "What do you do?"

So long ago that I was small & no one thought to ask "What do you do?" – the flash of friends like fireworks in the sky burned into the chambers hidden inside my eyes - the secret room where sunlight or fireworks are caught like phosphorescent shadows on a science-center wall.

My friends stayed on those inner chambers of the eye. I could not blink them away even when we fought & I tried so - for their thoughts were mingled with my thoughts. When I fell asleep I wondered what they might be doing & when I woke up I was a teen & older still.

They faded & were replaced by new friends made of, and through, smoke, before they were replaced by phone calls, before we all turned into Christmas cards & our first lives became jokes told by each other to each other's children.

Before we forgot how tricycles, in unison, creak out of lumber yards, the sweet smell of the lumber, the band-aids on our knees, small blue & gray coats against the sun –O– the way we did not speak but, like spring geese, turned as one and circled deep into back alleys.

Before, in short, we grew up.

I knew there was something I should remember into grown-up days / a simple poem.

I ask that small boy on a tricycle – Where are the babies?

He stops so quick & sharp that there is a pile-up of tricycles & as the boys pick themselves up/ as wheels are spinning in the sun the small boy that was me pitches light as thistle-down upon his feet & turns to squint at me as if I'm the sun.

He looks me in the eye and says – I may not tell.

You must remember on your own what lies behind the chill when the phone rings & it's your parents & why, in the deep of night, you sit upright in bed & cannot remember a word. Not a single image of what it is the dream-catcher did not catch. & while you catch your breath. I need to ride my tricycle. This is something we all need to do alone & together...

...& then, join me in the lumber yard for it is far away from home. It's a place where you're left alone. A place where you are safe.

The friends from my years-of-the-twenties-booze-ups sometimes still phone. "We're on a tear, and thought of you. When are you coming home – just for a visit?

But I grew into thirties and became busy & my face hid inside the pages, thru the suppressed rages, thru the 'I-can-help-you-tho-I-can't-help-myself' years that lingered into my forties when the tears fell & there was no longer any place to have a tear, except inside torn hearts. And then I aimed towards Seattle, and beyond.

That's why we allow the slow dripping of tears to enclose and encapsulate the beating lines of a Gargoyle Poet. We are eased to stillness, and are always shattered awake by falling shards of heart beats.

Dyad Moon

Where the gargoyle poet unraveled into life & prepared for Salt Spring's forest was Los Angeles, where Gargoyle executives are propped in the corners of board rooms, or driven in limos. They visit sets and say Harrumph. Replace writer after writer and say Harrumph.

Before he wrote of babies; before remembering the big snow that swept away the MockingBird Motel, & before faces forming in clouds are buried in the smog & before scripting mountains & how all mountains are walking giant women who lie down to sleep making green pastures green & how all the giants died & left their bodies to be mountain ranges & all knitted humans walk in the breasts of these giant women of the past who exhale clouds & the sky holds these clouds & that's where babies come from – O - a change was required.

Granny Knitwit and the cloud women make all things possible. Life blows thru us, and blows away children and parents; childhood, and wise hearts.

O, magical Clouds are breathed by giant women & in their wombs are clouds of warm-rich-rolling-blood-waves of a soft world that makes a blood-nest, a rich home & a rest to hold a baby-hand & roll a baby laughing with mist forming a baby to match each baby that the giant women of the mountains sigh.

Before the Gargoyle poet could say that – he had to shout:

Here am I in Los Angeles/ watching angels fly in brown rust we call the sky.

Where are you?/ Please tell me!

Who are you? / Please tell me.

In LA there's a hiss of paint spray & two artists tag their magic signs upon a wall. Long sultry names & rococo-curled names.

They're a gargoyle couple, who waited for Americans. When they woke up, the place was full & their gargoyle babies were missing.

His stone boots are polished & her fluorspar-stranded hair is polished & their eyes shine so very bright. Her language sparkles into the night. Culverts framed with diamonds which are hidden inside them the same way coins & straws & buttons hide in pancake dough on Shrove Tuesday.

The spray-paint is another finger, spray-pointed at the moon. The moon has curled like dried pancake dough hiding in the culvert. Culverts are the best poems of the city. City light.

The Gargoyle-Poet's Jaw creaks and hinges split, and flesh forms, and words form the tongue:

Huge balloon letters give life to buildings that creak the jaws of young men and women until they begin to yell.

Let the smell of spray as sweet as airplane glue inside used condom plastic-looking saran wrap all held by glue hanging the World-War-Two model planes in a cat-gut filament heaven that hung my four-year-old room twisting cat's gut planes that swayed with tremble of footsteps as she, my care-giver, of the ripe name came towards a bed - a small boy's bed and lifted the sheets and slid beneath, the bed-covers tipping in angles that cut and scratched; let that smell of spray mist on a summer day smear your hot cheeks.

The planes swayed & the strings tangled with the creaking of my narrow bed.

The sweet, nose-closing glue days mix with the true smells of spray paint and gasoline & exhaust smells even better with lots of oil in it. A tire burns the street & drips smoke that makes the painter poets grin and suck deep.

Before I was a small stone boy lying in different beds, before I hurt and rocked in my pebbled-pain at four-years-old -::- before my legs hurt from that same pain of the heart and I could wrap all my hurting in book-leaves -::- before I lay in bed in the forest -::- before I lay on leaves & looked up at the sky & wondered how fast we were really flying...

Before I looked up & knew there was no "up" & refused in school to agree that earth up-ended north tho' the world was round - before & because I would not agree that one thing was better than another & before and because I started to forget my name – why, before then, it became time for me to spray-paint this story into family albums/ to day-glo it on dumpsters/ to look deep in the ocean for it to bring the hard hands & the soft hands to make this story/ to bring the open hearts & the closed hearts & the soft eyes & the hard eyes & the wide eyes & the narrow eyes to tell this story...

Before the Train's last whistle.

It is time for Gargoyle-Artists to leave the asphalt. From the trees they hear the sound & in the forest there's the sound of missing stone children. Pianos are left behind, and float down stream, or get caught on reefs. Fish-bowl dwellers push against the sides, and slam stone-hands until glass shatters and they spill into the room of a big house. We run from dogs, and ride dangerous horses. We bleed what little money is needed just to live, and still keep writing our way to and with the river.

All of us? Artists – just like you. Everyone needs to find their missing babies.

Our stone-hearts hurt & eyes are burn in the sun. We're tumbling in time's streams. Our eyes steaming our tears. Gems in a muddy river, all of us.

And my helping hands feel like twin numb hearts beating/ beating/beating/ the room fills with white light & the walls dissolve with love & her heart still hurts & my head beats beats & even a gargoyle will slowly cross arms to hide the heart.

Fireworks fade & skid down the sky. Last sparklers light the chalkboard with smeared chalk.

We're losing babies & everywhere we turn there's more lost babies.

I've lost baby sisters.

I have lost baby brothers.

But because they're not near & because a deeper forest calls & because there are more babies & these babies are hidden in the forest - Why & When & Whereof, and What & thereof & either/or & more, though I am not a boy-child now, I move this fall-time body into the forest where there's no snow, no fireworks just a dusting of light ash.

Mead Moon

My body is the dog that won't be trained. Late at night, a time of beer & sawdust in conversation metaphysical about the ear & if no person's in the forest can the noh-person hear the sound of a falling tree -?- in the midst of all that, the dog that won't be trained has to go and take a piss upon that tree.

And when I bring my body back like a bone that won't let go, the pub has cleared and *time please* is the call. At night alone the bone is back & the dog will go and fetch it but won't let go until the bone is buried.

The dog that won't be trained makes me punch the piano. The dog that can't be trained has such hearing that the city rolls away and there's the sound of baying against an empty moon.

Where are you?

There are no drifts, just the rushing of an autumn stream. I cross another freeway - what did you look like? - to carry chunks of concrete into the bramble that leads to an off-ramp river, far past the cardboard homes beneath the overpass - did I hold you? - past the man who pisses in his trousers when I nod hello.

– Must feel good – I say & cause it does, he smiles, and pisses some more, spinning, wet & yellow & warm on a bridge in Los Angeles. O, he's crazy, say drivers – & they drive & break & break & drive, and wind up windows to stay very cool.

Driving past those who curl near shopping carts.

Did you visit me when you died?

As I listen to my breath. I feel rain upon my head. Face scratched and cut. I stop and reach into the mud. Because it is night time because the rain becomes a shiver of fog because my eyes burned and smoked and leaked dry tears when I was a little boy this work hurts.

Now I am a lone Gargoyle. Time-winds took me apart, took apart my gargoyle love, and everywhere we turned people no longer saw us. Might as well become part of a cliff again. Home by the quartz sea.

Seems we're part of the earth again & again.

But, somehow, I still write.

Wort Moon

Here is what Gargoyle Poets say:

1: Some babies have been hidden in the forest.

2: Some babies are buried in mudslides, next to a strong river. Because the rain has soaked my clothes, because the fog has shivered through my clothes I take my clothes off & stand next to the river watching my trousers shirt socks & underwear unfold & tumble downstream.

One hand scoops mud.

My other hand digs deep into the ground feeling for a baby arm - a baby leg - a baby shoulder. Steam rises from my chest. I must build a slippery wall made of mud and dead babies/ a mud-and-baby wall/ a wall of muddy deep dead babies & with this wall I make words to say right at the beginning - to be able to say - thank you Mothers of this earth/ thank you Mothers who breathed cloud babies & spray paint & glue & gasoline & toenails & fingernails & pencils & paper.

Thank you, for the skin of dust - thank you, for the feet of clay, the toes of rock, thanks to the weaver of blood-web-words, thank you for the DNA of language & thank you for all we know that lies under us & that's why we write our words...

... 'Tis to be like you & that's why we write to you or kill each other so we may be buried in you, become rolling seeds again. That's why we allow old age to take us, Mother, into your hands again - & why you breathe us out again as babies & that's why it's time I set this down, 'cause you've given me dreams that hold texture and color to the world for one sweet while so I may feel my heart beat against another's heart...

...So I may feel another's heart beat against my heart.

Oh, no one is beautiful & no one is ugly & no one is no one. I am hot with the gift of all breathing & I fly with it.

I am not a sparrow, nor an albatross, nor a bird of vivid rippling plumage.

Here is the kind of bird I am -::- not all my feathers are alike -::- not all of them will, wondrously black as raven, cut the sky when I enfold the clouds. I look down and see babies tumble in the stream; tumbling like bright pebbles -::- beach glass spun by Pacific waves -::- pebbles from the Boulder mountains.

Mom, I say to my knitted mother (knitted by her mother and by her great-grandma who lived with the fairies) I say to mom, in the room where the phone rarely rings...

...mom, I ask, in the room where only I know how deeply we now speak...

...can I write about my lost and tumbled away brothers & sisters?

She says... "...for the first time I feel I know you."

 I say to my mother. - Me too –

There's not another word that night. We look at each other, our eyes fill, and babies swim in her tears.

This is why we talked.

-::-

One small boy is caught in the center of the stream. Twigs, rocks, moss tangle about him until the stream fills with mountain flash-flood.

And he tumbles, tumbles, tumbles.

Barley Moon

In my child-hooded room when the night-light was clicked off & darkness undressed & descended/ & descending/ found its way inside my child-hooded heart/ my nostrils closed like a fist/ squeezing the cave-dark night & clutching the blackness & pulling it inside my heart & it flared like a dying star & that became another feather.

And I'd forgotten/ how to spell/ how to read/ how to let my ears hear/ my eyes see/ my tongue taste/ & all the letters jumbled in my head & face/ because I could/ not spell/ & I am being hit because I can/ not spell &/

/ all the light went with the falling hand

&

the hand had its own life & not the life of my father's eyes & brain/ his eyes had nothing to do with his falling hand/ which tore his heart/ but the tearing could not stop the arc & the descent - the regularity/ the spelling-bee flight/ his hand was swung by his father's eyes & his father's eyes were hard because of his own father's mouth. Stone hands. Gargoyle fingers.

I never deserted him, every moment leading up to and into his death I knew he was who he was.

I showed up one time he was supposed to have died. His eyes lit and beamed my way...and he started to say what he meant to say about what he should have done or not done, and...

...dad, who gives a shit? say I. Screw 'should' say I, don't talk to me about crap words like *should*.

His eyes still fill with tears.

Our eyes spin wet yarn strung from eye to eye. Stone pupil to stone pupil.

History no longer burns my body. Night no longer burns my chewed-over as-licorice feathers as sticky as melted black jelly-beans.

Black feathers, Raven feathers dripped my body with night/ beautiful night welcomed me when my tears caught fire & burned inside a nest/ inside its feathers & the night stroked my cheek like a black velvet Elvis Presley/ like a black and silver Madonna/ like a black & silver & golden & blue Mary

&

...when I touched my heart to black velvet it made dark flames & that smoke was as wonderful as tire smoke & I sucked that night inside my spine & spread my other black feathers.

Wine Moon

The Gargoyle Poet, turned first to yarn, next to wool-flesh, & then added all other colors to the black becoming a bird clothed with many feathers – O - his claws have paint on them.

It's night again & he flies above the city that's lit by tiny beacons of light turning from inside houses, joining flames near dumpsters.

Babies are swaddled in wax clothing. Their heads are wicks.

Flames ripple & parents' voices in lullaby city voices crackle with the flames. *You are a precious song* they sing in night's deep voice - Where are the baby songs!? - The parents' songs say - you are a precious song and that is why we sing you.

The city is filled with songs from suburbs, lover's houses dusted with fine snow-ash of canyon fires. Parents are tucking earthquake babies in earthquake homes, into earthquake beds, sheets of earth are covering canyon roads, tucking them in like sweet asphalt babies.

You are a precious song, they sing to the flying poet & the sun is warm upon his back, and morning rolls in & he lands in the forest.

Blood Moon

A car speeds thru childhood. A car is speeding thru fog.

A gray car is fast inside gray fog until it breaks through on a gray mountain road & the fog rolls back & spills into the valley & the car turns like a toy car in an awkward hand & breaks thru the fog & the 4-yr-old poet is in the backseat looking upside down at a moon bouncing in the window.

Time is taking another baby from his mother but he's not supposed to notice.

Where is this baby? And Granny Knitwit knits me into my story. My fingers on the keys, yarn to my fingers. She spins my woolen heart around my fingers. Stone fingers type in mitts.

The Gargoyle Poet Remembers everything
His voice stone-toned...

... I ask what is happening?

Nothing I am told.

Nothing.

Sleep Little one. You're dreaming. - But my mother is crying! Why is she crying? –

And another nite and another moon, and my mother is crying again, and Mildred Earle strokes her forehead, and I remember.

Even then I am a poet, and I look at mom's tears, and babies swim down her cheeks, and splash out the window. It is raining babies.

Shhhhhhhhh.... She cries because.... sometimes a mother cries...

...Listen to the moon while we tell you stories. My mother is crying. And no one will listen.

It's all fine, baby boy. The world is a happy place - We'll tell you stories about this happy place/ see the moon – well, mister moon has a face and that face is smiling.

I don't want stories! Stories are blankets & stories are pillows & stories are teddy bears.

Shhhhhhhhhh go to sleep.

How long should I sleep!!!!!??????

You should sleep all your life.

Snow Moon

Before & because I bring you my dead brothers & sisters before...

&

...because they bring you to me & because I killed them with my blood trail...

&

...because my dusty blood & the gritty anti-bodies of my blood made in my mother's body killed my siblings this bloody anti-body now stopped in time's body. O - no longer a baby now a falling writer's-body, now-on-fire-with-words aging & spinning body singing/screaming.

The song is of Rh positive & Rh Negative.

Stone jaws, blood sinews, hands dusty, nails golden in setting sun. I miss a roof-ledge. I sit so still.

Oh yes little one something was wrong and you did know all the secret heart of stories because I have to tell this to the world.

You must - say the giant women - You must, (O, sweet the breath of these women as their bodies roll me in new water, stone melts into pebbles, and naked boy again, I roll in words, I am washed by word-waves & I climb out and bare-feet walk in their green pastures - as their green pastures grow above me - as they now pin me with stars on nite's blanket.)

My Mother brought me my true red-headed sister, tho' together we were crying in different homes. She was carried to me. Placed on the ledge of my heart.

She who was lifted thru the clouds of dust on a windy road from one house to the house of my mother and father, and to me, so happy that I was no longer alone in the house of frozen childhood.

Now we hold each other's hand, and we weep babies, looking for our mother. Like Hansel and Gretel.

I look her in the eye. *Fuk DNA* I say to my sister. She laughs. *Fuk DNA* sez she.

Then the witch who made the candy-house hugs us.

And she guides me to one side of the casket of our mother, and I am there at the crossroads of the world with my sister and with my wife as witnesses, and with my nieces calling the compass, we lower my mother to the earth together in Gander, New found land, where babies find their parents, and where family gathers.

Thank you Mother Earth for my mother, thank you Mother Earth for my father. And time and earth will turn them towards each other, spinning with all of us.

Spinning.

You must - say the giant women, speak the truth.

I have something I must tell my children & readers. Look at me, my old babies, look at your father. I must tell you. I have rushed across railway tracks with the train coming.

- I can make it - said I to Les Stoodley once upon a different time. - Jesus, we made it - said Les Stoodley to me one second later as the train roared behind us. Now dead he still almost made it, till the time-train came around the curve to take him & because I'm still on my way along death's path, I've made it this far.

We all made it. But O how every one of us partied along the way.

The Knit-witted poet says...

I admit my life to my children.

I have driven my car at top speed into icy flooded gravel pits. I have smoked opium and danced with wild women. I have munched on cacti. O, I have driven to the moon.

I admit this to my children.

I have held firm to a spinning porcelain toilet of the ceiling as it spun and vomited words.

I admit this to my children.

I have looked at my muscles and found them wanting - at my heart and found it wanting.

I admit all to my parents

My mother, diminished in size, but translucent, lay on a lucent bed. Light poured, in her 90s, from her mouth and eyes. She became a nova. A terra nova.

On these high holy days of a poem. I admit to all of you just who I am / my stone jaw shatters in front of my children and I admit that they are my parents/ and also my children/ think of any sin & I have done it & think of any good and I have done it/ they are dancing in a place/where I have never/ danced or smelled the rosin/ all are spray-painting/ in the corners of my heart and I did not always know when they were there but when they rippled into Pele's pumice I once hurt but now I heal.

When they burned the nest, I, the Gargoyle poet, watched smoke rising above my eternal tipi. "That's just how it is," sez mom. The phone was still. "Everyone is free," sez mom to me & me to mom.

We sit and say nothing in her long-term room, and I tell her the true story of my life, and she tells me her true story.

Day after day, night after night, and in silence we knit the day. In silence we knit the night.

I walk down the hall. My stone feet used to slam the floor. Now I walk quietly with knitted-feet.

I had the cash of a poet, so I stayed till I could no more, and went away, and then returned on airline points and cash. Away and back; back and away.

Dad tugs the yarn, and turns me and mom towards Signal Hill.

- Oh look - we say as a cloud spins past the window.

This is the song from the seconds-away time when I become a gargoyle father with open mouth and dry tongue; when I become the dad who is motionless as a rock upon a burning beach & am burning into ashes to ashes & this is for when I'll be born smiling at last into the earth mother/ & when I am born again into the sky mother/& when the water and fire mothers/ cut deep into my back and open the wing slits and pull them out again for when they unfurl me and I sail through the sky with all my dead brothers and sisters.

I thought I had dreamed them and they had dreamed me.

This is their story because my tongue has been kissed by crooked angels and my body is changing into something new. This is for when I'm the father who can't stay away from my words.

I am the father & son who farts, burps, picks dry snot and flicks it at the sky, who could love all the world but doesn't; who could give you his heart but now keeps it close & this is the father & the son who let you play with his shadow.

This is your father who cries at night and laughs there too.

This is your cousin who has screamed inside his heart because it was the quietest place.

I'm flying over you. Past all places I've ever been.

My claws are dipped in paint. My claws are dipped in oil. My claws are spray painted. My claws are ringing metal & of glass.

There's nothing to fear.

One feather of my poet wings, is my grandmother Alice, another is my grandmother Suzanne & another is my great-grandmother Julia & another is my Aunt Em & another part of my ear is a cup on string when spun SHOUTing SINGing Cracking against an iceberg – that's only one molecule of my ear.

I swoop through readers' eyes, past the edge of pages, behind the pages that block the view of each room. I sprinkle salt and pepper words on a page, and you shake the page the way a prospector pans for gold.

When you set down this book, pick up your own, slam the keys, trace your fingertip along the screen, flick your own words across the street, chew gum while you sing. Throw your own book in the air, catch it and run down the street singing your song.

When you speak any word (any at all) that word has in it anyone who ever spoke it or ever read it & that word has in it letters and each letter contains all paragraphs all poems all the times anyone said fuck you or I hurt or oh do that again oh it feels so good do it again please.

When the mouth is filled with food & you want to swallow but you are crying & the food falls out and, O, sweet Jesus, ask the teeth and the tongue of Mary - Mother of God - of sky. O, cloud women of giant mountains what is to become of me???!!!

See the poem-bird fly by & it's spiraled with old tires it is encrusted with dried condoms and it is filled with cars & held by the sky & because and before it is held by language it is ready to swoop and turn and look you in the eyes and let you look in its eyes.

If you wish, say go away.

If you wish, kill and cook and eat it.

If you wish, fly with me on as variegated, as wild a flight yourself, as we zoom with the moon beneath us & the moon before us & it is time to fly this poem together & we sweat while we weld its wings with blood sparks. Oh I wing-spin & I fly in poem-bird flight through the sky.

The Piano bobs in choppy inky seas. Sharpening a finger with a chisel I dip the nail into the ocean, and write along the keys. Granny Knitwit sees I am born and knits herself into the moon. And stays. She knits one side while she unravels the other. She becomes the moon.

I am my father and I am my mother & I am my cousin & I am my own child.

Flying like a mile wide Raven I must wrap my claws around my self and because the world spins and because the world is still and because there are many maps and now I have found this one to be made of cloud cloth…because of all this, I must lift my wings & feel my back hurt & the wings are heavy on my back & I am back & here I am.

I fly above the St. John's railway station, to watch the Newfie Bullet arrive and leave at the same time.

O, know that all my friends and old relatives wait for me at the station, no matter how long or short a time it takes to get there.

I already hear people jawing, and playing cards, and laughing, and I will swoop to board the train again, and again, as long as there runs a train. Forever.

I am flying & beneath is a lumber-yard filled with tricycles and one spinning small boy who once was me looking with upright face into the sun.

His eyes are mine and I spin in those eyes as I fall to earth. I don't care if I wobble. I don't care if I plummet.

I don't care if I soar & I don't care if I die & I dance in the air & you are my partner....

... &

...We, once again – rocks rolling down a slope – are bouncing planets in a funnel, seeing-eye story-dogs; gripping granite-fingers curl and creak and break. Rock snakes squirm away – all ten of them.

Closing Shots:

The gargoyle has shattered.

Light leaks out like yolk from cracked eggs.

O, my eyes are mica, eggshell-shattered drifted in front of the feet of statues.

I see the sun.

The sun is shadow. My heart cracks open, the gargoyle shattered. O…

…we all…again…poem after poem…

All of us…

    fall

        fall

           fall

              and rise together.

The End

Roll Credits

After Words: Acknowledgements & all that:

The stories in my linked Urban Fables *"Tales Of A Small Boy In A Big Room"* became part of this meta-work-that's-been-in-progress since 1972. All linked in the long-term room where my mother watched Signal Hill and when I read her part of a poem... she kept looking at the hill and said - read more.

All stories mutated into this mind-movie in 2017, having been swung round by one of my sea-anchors – the Terra Nova Rock, and then moored next to the rocks of the BC Coastline. Back and forth...free rides, couch surfing as my mother approached night-time. Five years ago I realized that chunks of my *Bloodsparks* book had grown wings, and so that book flew to the meeting place of poem-birth & was absorbed by Gargoyle poets.

Some portions were issued as poems/plays in collections such as: *31 Newfoundland Poets* (*Breakwater Books*)/ *East Of Canada*. (*Breakwater Books*)/ *The Proper Lover*. (*Hounslow Press*)/*CyberKind* (*Internet Publication*) & as part of my contribution to *'answers to unmailed letters'* (Santa Monica Playhouse) read aloud at various Boulder Theatre readings/ chanted during readings at Goddard College/ given away in street readings in Boulder & readings given in St. John's Newfoundland.

These fables have been worked on in Nain, Labrador/St. John's, Nl/Boulder, Co/San Francisco, in its own state/Washington DC/as well as on our rented '57 Chris-Craft off Stockholm Island, BC/and in our Tipis & Trailers & shacks on Salt Spring Island, as well as in our Kits nest & also at Battery Road when we lived there in 2007.

Thanks as far back as the sixties, when I'd sit with my friends Adrian Fowler and his sister Rosalie as they sang and we traded thoughts and leaned towards the songs together.

The full kettle of yarns continued to brew at *Café Sole* & *Boulder Book Store Coffee Shop* & *The Laughing Goat* & *Salt Spring Roasting Company* & *Jumping Bean* in St. John's & various *Tim Horton's* outlets around Canada. Thanks to all for allowing us table space. Coffee is wonderful medicine for Gargoyle Poets.

Thanks to Michael Kanaly for assisting me, as always, with the cover's final details & for being a friend & to Pat O'Flaherty for his encouragement & insights & friendship over the years & once again to Joe Partington for notes and responses, and to both Joe & Hope for providing a happy place to couch-surf. Thanks to Larry Mirkin for reading my poems and writing to tell me what he felt about what he read. Thanks for Goddard College for, decades ago, welcoming me. Thanks to my dad's cuz-squad who became my source 'on-the-rock' family. Thanks to Fritz Arnold, who understood the poetry of objects.

I am grateful to the always resourceful Vicky Phillips for aiming me towards Goddard, and to Nora Mitchell, Poet, for helping me land. And for encouraging my poetry; evoking it.

Thanks to Indy filmmaker Paul McGowan for always finding a place for us on his land, and to our buddy Sky, for saving our butts on various occasions. Thanks to Mom for listening to me read this aloud. Always encouraging, she never suggested I get 'a real job' – she knew exactly what I do.

Thanks to Ashley & Dave & Marilyn & Clarence, & Dave & Penney & Aunt Eileen & Caren's family & our dear friend Teal. They all rescued me. Thanks for your phone calls to ask how I was doing.

Thanks to Pat and Ken Lyons for welcoming me into their Family and making me feel at home, when I most needed to feel at home. Thanks to Cori & Darren & families for their caring ways.

Many thanks to Sax Francisco for offering room to pitch at the *Eclectic Tea Room*, and to colleague & buddy Maryke McEwan for offering space for a nomadic poet when I hit town.

Once I could never swear near mom. But, as the end of her life appeared and she heard the stories about me, she smiled when I said 'Bullshit.' She knew I was, as Jim Murphy calls me... "Wild Bill" and she'd become rather proud of that. When she was 93, a homeless friend said to her, "I fucking loves you, Ruby." And she smiled. And reached out to squeeze his hand.

The world gives back what it takes. At the end of her life Mom wheeled down the hall and into Wisdom. Her wheels skidded on light.

&

as we fade to black...many thanks to you, for reading my books & attending these mind-movies. Thanks for riding this phantom train.

Remember; it will stop anytime you wave it down, no matter where it is; no matter who you are. The Newfie Bullet gives rides to anyone who flags down the train. It invites *all* passengers to ride.

All.

Time to close the curtains.

All Aboard.

All aboard your very own time-train.

gull pond books

Gull Pond Books :

Novels:
The Terra Nova Quartet:
Maud's House
Chips & Gravey
Midnight At The Mockingbird Motel
This Is What I Must Remember

"The Newfie Bullet" Trilogy
My Newfie Bullet
Poet In A Pontiac
Dogs Of A Strange Town

Poetry
Ocean Of Childhood
Shinto Poem Field
Moon Tides

Mystery Series:
Panama Kills!
LA Kills (Summer 2017)
Washington Kills! (Fall 2017)

Children's Books:
The Adventures Of Stumpman